Nouveau Haitiah

Donald McEwing

3/16

Leon

INTRO

Breaking through the surface of warm water and gasping for breath, I kicked and splashed and turned in near panic. Where was I? Realizing my feet could touch the sandy bottom, I made my way to the edge of the pool and crawled out, coughing and spluttering, and collapsed upon a narrow strip of black sand beach bordered by yellow grass.

Wavelets lapped against my pale skin and soaking wet safari clothes. I pushed myself to my hands and knees and crawled, with my long brown hair hanging about my face in sodden strands. Grounding my feet in the yellow grass beneath me, I slowly unrolled into a standing position and surveyed my surroundings.

The circular pool was surrounded by dense jungle vegetation- palms, cycads, tall ferns, and more. Every gradation of purple colored the leaves and fronds, from bright purples to dark ones, to violet, lavender, and lilac pastels, with the other dominant foliage color being yellow. Bushes with large leaves furled into funnels looked like pitchers designed to trap and drown prey in the pool at their bottom.

The air was warm and humid, and tinged with an odor of charcoal and anise.

Next to the o-shaped pool, a small metallic blue beetle with eight legs crawled from a crack in a damp rock and focused its attention upon me.

A flock of yellow and carmine creatures flew low across the palms. They looked like no birds I had ever seen, all wings and legs, but no apparent tails. Overhead, a high purplish-gray overcast filtered a small yet intense sun.

I was experiencing *jamais vu*. I must have been here before, but everything appeared utterly unfamiliar, as if I were seeing it for the first time. I could not remember my past. All my memories had been washed away. What happened in that pool?

A sealed grey urn sat on the sand nearby. On its side it said 'Leon.'

"That's me," I said aloud. The urn looked like the kind used for cremated ashes. I picked it up, broke the seal, and opened it. I was afraid it would contain something gruesome, like ashes and bones. It turned out there were ashes after all, but not human ones; the urn contained the ashes of a book. A corner of one page had failed to burn, but the words were illegible. Fire had reduced the individual letters to mere random symbols on what once was a beautiful creamy page. *"Sorry it is dark in there!"* I thought as I closed and resealed the urn.

It was warm, and my skin quickly developed a fine sheen of perspiration. A breath of a breeze blew through the canopy of purple-hued palms, and the jungle leaves seemed to sigh as they shook, a gentle riffling like the turning of pages. Dry stems rattled overhead, and high above, the wind blew through the fronds. The front pocket of my wet shirt contained a lump, which turned out to be a soggy petite madeleine. The small cake smelled like the trampled grass beneath my feet, like ashes and anise. I shrugged, and tossed it into the bush. *"The jungle will recycle it,"* I thought.

From nearby, rustling in the bushes made it seem as if the jungle itself were alive. The leaves at the edge of the clearing parted and a portly young man emerged, dressed in a stained and faded green graduation gown. He was short and dark skinned, with a broad nose, round cheeks, and kinky black hair. He was sweating profusely, and his voice was high pitched. He stopped to catch his breath and addressed me. *"Bonjour!* I'm glad to see you! Who are you? Are you a colonialist?"

"A colonist?"

He pursed his lips and rubbed his chin. He looked confused. "You don't look like you come from around here. Do you come from Combray?" His face brightened. "Are you a doctor?"

"No."

His features fell in disappointment. "Well, we need a doctor."

6

I wanted to be helpful. I felt obliged to show I cared, and if someone needed saving, I would be glad to try. "Is it an emergency?"

He rolled his eyes. "It's always an emergency."

"I know some first aid."

"*Bon.*" He said with finality. That apparently settled the matter for him. He glanced at the urn. "What's that?"

"An urn."

"What's inside?"

"Ashes."

He made the sign of the crossroads, quickly touching his forehead, heart, each shoulder, and then pointing towards the ground and sky. I did not tell him the ashes came from a book, rather than a human. What difference did it make? Having made his obligatory observance, he sniffed dismissively. "Too bad it's not a canteen. That would have been useful. Where are you taking it?"

"Combray," I answered with a shrug.

He laughed. "Forget Combray. It is a long way from here. Follow me."

He turned to re-enter the jungle. I squinted at the blue-white sun overhead. The heat was intense. Humidity kept my thin white shirt plastered to my chest and back. I looked back at the pool; a fine layer of dust had already covered the surface. On the other side of the pond, reeds grew around the perimeter, and the water flowed from an outlet. I could hear the musical sound of a small waterfall coursing down rocky shale on the other side. He stepped into the bush, and I followed, carrying the urn. We were atop a low hill, so the beginning of the trek was downhill.

Although the corpulent orderly dismissed a journey to Combray, right then and there I promised myself I would go. He thought I came from Combray, so that must be where I belonged. I should go to Combray. Besides, the urn had my name on it, and the proper thing to do with an urn filled with ashes was to make a journey and scatter them. I introduced myself, and asked his name.

"Remy." He was already breathing hard. "By the way, welcome to Nouveau Haitiah." He pronounced it 'hay-sha.'

"Thanks," I said dryly.

"We should hurry."

Judging by his huffing and puffing, I would have no problem keeping up with him. "Where are we going?"

"Camp," he replied. "Near Bois Caiman. It's about eight miles."

What was I getting into? I brushed aside an overhanging frond. The foliage was becoming thicker, so less sunlight was reaching the ground. Remy pushed ahead.

"Is this really an emergency?" I asked. "I am not a doctor."

"If you know first aid, then you're a doctor. I am sure you will know more than anyone else; besides, our last doctor died of a fever." He wiped sweat from his brow. "If we hurry, we'll get to camp before sundown. Come on. We need to be there before the soldiers return." He walked in silence for a few steps. "You don't look like a fighter."

"I am not."

"Me neither."

I was always tall and thin, but stronger than I looked, with dark hair, dark eyes, and graceful hands and long fingers. When it came to doing anything, I used to joke 'these hands are meant to read books.' But this situation was far beyond anything I had ever read about. The heat was incredible, the humidity suffocating. Did he say I did not look like a fighter? I licked my lips. "Do you have anything to drink?"

"No."

I did not appreciate the abruptness of his reply. Now I knew why he said the urn would have been more useful if it had been a canteen. We walked for a while without speaking. The gravel and black sand crunched beneath my feet.

Finally, Remy called back to me. "Don't tell the others you're not a doctor. It will be better for you." I am pretty sure what he really meant was 'it will be better for me,' but I let the matter drop, because just then a small, metallic blue, eight-legged amphibian startled me as it hopped across the trail and back into the bush.

"What was that?" I asked. "I have never seen anything like it."

He shrugged without turning around.

"Tell me about the local flora and fauna."

"Flora? Fauna? What are those?"

I took a deep breath and tried again. "Tell me about the plants and animals."

"What's to tell? Don't mess with them."

"What about that frog thing?"

"I don't know," he said irritably. "Leave it alone."

"OK. What do I need to know? Which animals are dangerous?"

He stopped and looked me up and down. "You really don't know, do you?" I shook my head.

He patted me on the shoulder. "That's what comes from city living. The bush is a lot different from Combray." I agreed wholeheartedly. I was beginning to like the sound of this Combray. His hand was still on my shoulder, and I noticed his fingernails were dirty and ragged.

"Well, my friend," Remy said, warming to the idea of demonstrating his expertise, "the most dangerous animals are the crapaud bouga. They're big- almost as big as a man- and they're fast, and they're smart. Most animals are slow, but not the big toads. You almost never see them, though."

"Good."

"Oh! Annies are very slow, but if those worms catch you on the ground, then it's all over. What a bad way to go! The white whips in the rivers and ocean are very dangerous. Don't go in the water. Other than that, you should be fine." Remy said this with great finality.

"What about the plants?" I asked.

He chuckled. "They won't hurt you."

"Can I eat them?"

"No. Only eat food grown in towns or fenced fields." Remy appeared to consider the matter. "They're all parasites."

"The plants or animals?"

"Both. Everything eats each other."

My stomach rumbled. "Speaking of eating, what should I do for a meal? I have no food and I have no money."

He laughed. "Me neither. We'll eat when we get back to camp. Hope you like red beans and rice. By the way, you are now in the Lord's Army of Resistance- the LAR- commanded by the great Lord Waterman. Congratulations!"

"An army?" I asked with alarm. "I am not a fighter. What is all this about soldiers and fighting?"

"The fighting never ends," he answered. "Around the towns people keep to themselves. The women grow food and raise children, except for a few like Victoria. Most of the fighting is in the jungle. Men fight."

"Why? What are they fighting for?"

"I don't know. Maybe they just like fighting. I'm only an orderly. You're the doctor. Why don't you do something about it?"

OVERTURE

The light faded, and the jungle gave way to wide
meadows of yellow spear grass. The encampment of
Bois Caiman became visible, and it was little more
than a collection of tents arranged around a central
clearing. Two young men stood watch along the path
of trampled grass leading to the camp's center.

"You!" Remy called to them. "Yes, you!" Light the
torches! I found a doctor! How can he save anyone if
he doesn't have enough light to see?"

They ran off to obey. Soon, black smoke rose from the
guttering flames into the hazy twilight. The sun went
down, and eight-legged lightning bugs rose over the
dry fields of spear grass, flashing blue bioluminescent
calls to potential hosts. Despite my disorientation, I
thought the flashing little lights over the meadow
were one of the prettiest sights I had ever seen.

The orderly and I made our way through the nearly
deserted camp. Voices drifted to me from across the
meadow. The Lord's Army of Resistance soldiers were
returning. I could make out a flag at the head of their

ragged procession, a black diamond upon a yellow field, now hanging motionless from its staff. The silhouetted band of hunched figures followed the standard as they passed an abandoned and collapsing colonial Habitation. They carried several casualties.

The dirty, disheveled soldiers entered camp. Their blood was up; they were loud and waving machetes and going on about an ambush by the Children's Fund faction. The wounded were brought to the broad open area in the middle of the encampment; it was going to serve as a triage station.

This presented a dilemma for me. I had no tools to work with, literally nothing; there was not a scrap of metal to be found! It turned out metals were rare, but fortunately, one mineral was plentiful: black diamonds. They provided a cutting edge like no other, so black diamond machetes were commonplace. But I was at a loss as to how to treat these people. Would infection even be an issue? I wanted to help, but these were incredibly primitive conditions; and yet, in all likelihood I probably did know more about first aid than these young men. It was too late to back out now. Wanting to save people was all well and good, but this was another thing entirely, and now lives depended on me. I had to try. And I was in way over my head.

For the time being, I set the urn off to the side, next to an unoccupied tent. I wiped my brow, pulled up my sleeves, and directed Remy to place the wounded on cots around the station.

"Could someone boil water," I asked. No one moved. No one other than Remy had even spoken to me since entering camp. It felt like a combination of indifference and disrespect, as if they accepted the notion that I was a doctor without question, but did not see a doctor as part of the Army.

The portly orderly smoothed his green gown with dirty hands. "Who first?" His ragged fingernails caught on the fabric, while the flickering torchlight cast strange shadows on his face, accentuating his round cheeks and chin, while deepening the creases in his brow, making his eyes appear sunken. Distant thunder rolled across the alien sky, and rippling sheets of heat lightning backlit the soft violet clouds. I hoped it would rain. The humidity was stultifying. In addition, small airborne pests kept biting. I shooed away one of the metallic red arachnoflies, surveyed the wounded, and took a deep breath. "That one," I answered.

I approached a rickety stretcher and knelt next to it to examine a young soldier. A large, dark bloodstain soaked the front of his coarse khaki shirt. It was neatly buttoned to the collar, with no sign of an entry wound. The nametag was barely legible: L'Overture. His feet drummed against the stretcher at an impossibly fast rate. An ankle bracelet of black diamonds clinked in time to his drumming feet.

I felt his neck- no pulse.

I leaned over and listened for breath- no respiration.

Remy wrung his hands in distress. "It's L'Overture. Can you save him?"

"No," I replied.

"But he's moving!"

"It is just discharging synapses, an electrical-"

"-What are you talking about? Help him!"

I sighed. I did not know what to do, but Remy knew even less than me, if possible. "All right," I said. "Let's take a look. I unbuttoned L'Overture's shirt and peeled away the sticky wet fabric. There was a hole in his chest. His heart had been removed. The incision was extremely clean; it must have been done with one of those black diamond machetes. After removing the heart, someone had re-buttoned the shirt.

I wiped the sweat from my brow with the back of my arm. The shock of seeing this fantastic cruelty, this atrocity, left me shaking. "Who did this?" I asked. Not that it really mattered. Dead is dead. I did not know what else to say.

"The Children's Fund," one of the soldiers answered.

"The barefoot witch, Odette," another added.

"They are cannibals. Commissar Ampere is the worst."

"Take this body away." As I moved towards the next cot I glanced back at Remy. He was rifling through the dead man's pockets. Remy pilfered a pair of orange and yellow octagonal dice that looked like they were formed from amber, and then waddled after me, smiling without a hint of apology. "Sooner or later," he said, "everyone rolls, and everyone gets rolled."

The man on the next stretcher, Toussaint, wore a shower cap and black pajamas. He rocked from side to side, groaning, his arms tightly wrapped around his gut. An LAR veteran called Coulomb stood next to the stretcher. Coulomb's eyes were bloodshot and, due to the ever present humidity, he was sweating copiously too. He was removing a ceramic canteen's stopper for his groaning friend.

"Water," the wounded man moaned. "Oh, have mercy. Water. I'm so thirsty."

"Wait!" I said to Coulomb, gesturing to his canteen. I remembered reading about stomach wounds in a book. Water would make the suffering worse. An old saying popped into my head: 'the soul migrates to water.'

"Please," he groaned. "I'm burning up. Water."

I knelt beside him, while Remy took up a position behind Coulomb. I touched Toussaint's forehead. He was burning up. I gently pulled his arms away from his stomach to examine the injury.

Knife wound-

Intestines badly scrambled-

Two vertical slashes and one across, like the letter 'H'.

"Oh, oh, oh water." His quavering voice hit a higher note with each 'oh.' Gripping his stomach, he resumed rocking.

I stood and faced the veteran. "He is done for," I stated with far more conviction than I actually felt. "It is only a matter of time. Do not give him anything to drink. It will only make his pain worse." I shook my head in sorrow.

"Water," the man moaned.

"Just a sip," Coulomb said.

"No!" Remy shouted. "You heard the doctor! Take him away and put him out of his misery."

Coulomb uttered a low growl and took a step towards me. His right hand dropped to his machete.

"Stop," Remy said from behind him. His tone halted Coulomb in his tracks. The veteran did not even turn to check if the orderly had a weapon. "Chief Harado from the Children's Fund did this to Toussaint, not our doctor."

"Leave him alone," another soldier called from the shadows.

"Oh, oh, oh."

I avoided looking at Toussaint. I could not save him. I did not have the knowledge or the tools, and even if I did, saving him seemed impossible. I shook my head. "He'll go on like this all night."

Remy addressed the veteran. "You know what to do. Put him out of his misery and cremate him. Do it now."

The veteran turned on me. "Damn you. All right. I'll do it." He spit on the dry ground and turned on me. "Curse you, doctor: may you know thirst the rest of your days." He hurled his canteen at me and missed.

I shook my head and licked my lips. Let Remy deal with him. Coulomb was right about one thing. My whole life I had been thirsty in the book sense of the word. I wanted to save these people. I wanted to save myself too. Suffering, disease, old age, and death had always threatened to wipe out everything that mattered, even memory. I thirsted for a painkiller, a miracle cure, a magical powder, a fantastical Fountain of Youth to restore, or better yet, transcend the loss that came with the human condition.

One thing was for sure: I was a long way from doing anything about it right now. For the time being, I would have to pretend. I would act like a doctor and attend to simple physical sufferings. I could do that much. I could apply a bandage or tourniquet or splint, or offer a drink of water. But I could not cure my own mundane middle-age aches and pains, never mind the horrendous injuries of L'Overture or Toussaint. Death trumped my efforts, right before my eyes. The amber dice were already cast. What could I do? Ah yes, 'do no harm' was a fine thing for a real doctor, but what if it amounted by 'do no good' or, in my case, simply not knowing what to do; well, what then? How could I save them? How could I save myself?

These burning questions haunted me as I made my way through the camp's makeshift triage station. Someone was kind enough to give me a bowl of rice and red beans, which I ate between treating patients. As I made my rounds, I found myself near the unoccupied tent where I had left the urn. I went to check it, and found something odd: someone had painted the urn. They had painted it in LAR colors, with a black diamond on a yellow background, and cross hatching for decoration, obliterating my name in the process. This made me angry. It was a kind of betrayal, since the urn was my connection with the pool, and I could not remember anything from before the moments when I crawled on my hands and knees onto that narrow strip of sand; however, the urn was still sealed and its contents undisturbed, and my situation demanded my full attention, so I let the matter go, and moved on. At last, I reached the last casualty. A tall, dark-skinned, muscular man lay motionless and unconscious upon a stretcher. It was a head wound, and there was a lot of blood. An enemy from the Children's Fund had impaled him with a machete, punching it straight down through his skull.

It was now sticking out of the top of his head, its hilt forming a macabre cross.

I knelt by the man's side and touched his neck- a faint pulse.

I listed for respiration, and incredibly, he was still breathing.

His nametag read 'Korpusant.' He wore loose-fitting black pajamas, an outfit both childlike and terrifying at the same time, and though he appeared young, his forehead was creased with deep wrinkles. I carefully probed the blood matted hair around his entry wound. No question; remove the knife, and Korpusant would quickly die. It was amazing he was still alive in the first place. Leaving the knife in his skull would only mean dying would take longer.

Soldiers gathered around us. They had already seen my failures to save L'Overture and then the man with the stomach wound, Toussaint, and they had seen Coulomb curse me. Now, emboldened by the safety of darkness and the anonymity of the crowd, they aimed their resentment at me. They shouted and whistled from the shadows beyond the torches, their calls mixing with the buzz of arachnoflies, chirping cycad hoppers, and overhead, the rumble of thunder and the flashes of heat lightning.

Remy came to my side and put his hand on my shoulder, but he could not protect me from their disrespect. He whispered in my ear: "A woman named Odette did this to Korpusant. See that hilt? Now the sign of the crossroads crowns his head."

"How could she be that strong?" I asked.

"Simple. She is the Children's Fund's witch."

I was momentarily overwhelmed by *jamais vu* again, a sense of disconnection, of never having been there. It all seemed utterly unfamiliar- Remy, Korpusant, the lightning bugs, the calls of the soldiers, this alien world.

A woman's voice rose above the unruly crowd. "You can save him."

Her voice pulled me back into this world of Nouveau Haitiah. I saw her, a young woman with erect posture and long, well-groomed black hair, short in height and slight in build. She wore a white shift, and I realized I

had seen her before- or perhaps I was experiencing
déjà vu? This woman seemed familiar. Behind her,
countless blue bioluminescent lights floated in the
field, constellations of stars, constantly shifting. The
men surrounding the woman appeared dumbfounded
by superstitious awe. Was she some sort of witch?

"Save him," she implored.

Thunder rattled across the fields. The heat lightning
rippled through the clouds again. It felt like the entire
world was a living organ animated by electricity.

I knelt by Korpusant and re-examined his wound.

"Save him," she repeated. The third time it was a
command, not a request. She crossed the trampled
spear grass to stand by my side. Her features were
fine and regular. Upon her delicate wrist she wore a
bracelet with small violet beads, with yellow and
brown comma-shaped dots upon each one. I
extended a hand and looked into her brown eyes. She
presented her cheek to me for a kiss, and whispered a
word in my ear, and a series of brief instructions on
what to do; at the same time, she pressed an object
into the palm of my hand.

"Who are you?" I asked. "Have we met before?"

"I'm Victoria." She withdrew her hand and faced the soldiers.

"The doctor will save Korpusant. His body is dead, but his mind still dreams. The doctor will raise him from the dead."

I surreptitiously examined the object Victoria had placed into my hand. It was small, with eight sides, and at first I thought it was an octagonal die, but the texture was all wrong. Upon closer examination, I discovered it was a grainy lump of purple crystals. It glittered in the flickering torchlight in a most attractive way. This must be diamond root.

Following her whispered instructions, I closed my fist and crumpled the lump into powder. Next, I bent down a snapped a tubular stalk of spear grass. Using the grass as a pipette, I leaned over Korpusant and blew the sparkling granules into his nose. I knew from the talk of the soldiers that this diamond root was a powerful drug. Despite my best efforts to avoid it, my tongue touched some of the crystals. I recognized the flavor of anise and ashes. It permeated this world.

The wounded man's hand twitched. His entire body convulsed, as if being shocked; he gasped, he gulped deep breaths, and at last, his eyes fluttered open. He focused upon my chest and then raised his eyes to meet my gaze. Korpusant drew a long shuddering breath. "I dreamed-"

"-Yes, you dreamed. Your mind dreams after your body dies." The taste of the diamond root was making me lightheaded. "You are back now," I continued. "You are back in camp."

"I dreamed about a Fountain of Youth."

Victoria returned, her white shift shimmering orange in the torchlight. She gestured with her hand, making the sign of the crossroads. A Christian would say it was the Stations of the Cross, but up to this point I had seen no signs of such worship, and many indications that superstition ruled. It appeared to be voodoo, or Santeria, and invoking the crossroads- according to some books, the intersection where the realms of life and death touch- seemed the most likely explanation. She confirmed my assumption by pointing up and then pointing down. She was acknowledging the intersection of the crossroads was three dimensional; it also extended vertically, like a black plume of smoke rising into the sky, as well as downward in the direction of the world's burning center. Furthermore, if one connected the six indicated directions, the resulting geometrical shape was an octagon, hence, the eight-sided dice. The dice carried additional symbolic freight because they were made from amber, a substance traditionally used to represent time; the word 'amber' actually gave rise to the word 'electricity.' For me, the symbols of the LAR and Nouveau Haitiah all came together in the person of Victoria, her powerful grace, and the amber octagonal dice.

My thoughts should have been completely focused, given the nature of my situation; and yet, despite these dire circumstances- attempting to act as a doctor while knowing little about medicine; attending to strangers in a strange culture; stranded in an even stranger alien world- despite all this, my thoughts wandered. Victoria's graceful gesture affected and distracted me. The diamond root was taking hold.

Somewhere deep within me, a powerful rush was building.

Meanwhile, Korpusant scanned the dumbfounded crowd from his stretcher. Apparently he recognized someone and, ignoring Victoria and me, rose from the stretcher. Reeling and staggering, he propelled himself towards his fellow soldiers, using his arms in a swimming motion, and made his way through the crowd. He smiled and laughed and shook hands with his comrades. Most were still too shocked by the gory sight of the machete projecting from the top of his head to react. Some whispered the word 'zombie.' Korpusant found the veteran, Coulomb, and gave him a hearty embrace. They were joined by several soldiers: a wiry, dark haired soldier, Private Current; a tall, handsome, dark-skinned man, Fernal; a short, stocky, thick necked trooper, Voltson; the quartermaster Faraday; and then another, a man who wore fashioned his hair in a crown of high spikes, and called himself 'Mister Liberty.' Leaning against one another, they moved into the shadows beyond the torchlight.

I covered my face with my hands. Disconnected thoughts tumbled one after another, while my body buzzed with the swelling music of the drug. What should I do? Korpusant would die soon. It was a matter of time. There was no way he could survive that wound, no way. He was beyond saving. Ultimately, the same was true for all of these LAR troops, the enemies over at Children's Fund, everyone. They would be eaten alive by the violence of their own culture. They were mere reflections of this planet's violent ecology, and there was nothing I could do to save them. Yet a sense of basic decency and compassion compelled me to try.

Remy cleared his throat and wiped his hands on the front of his green graduation gown. "Are you all right? Your eyes are dilated."

Victoria moved to stand by his side. "Well, witch doctor?"

Her hand grazed my arm. Her touch electrified me. It rooted me to the spot like a bodhi tree struck by lightning, and the electrical surge instantaneously transformed me into a conductor between the sky and ground. My dilated eyes opened to the world of Nouveau Haitiah and let it in. It now entered my perception without the overlying filters of judgment or ideational constructs, and it was overwhelming. I closed my eyes, but nothing could stop it now. My body rippled with the tremors of my mind's discharging synapses, until perceptions and sensations simultaneously imploded and exploded, back and forth, expanding in a feedback loop, filling my ears with crackling thunder and my eyes with heat lightning and my head with the smell of diamond root, ashes and anise. I shook with the earthquake of revelation-

And I saw the way.

THE NEXT DAY

Violent shaking awoke me.

"Wake up!"

I opened my eyes. Victoria loomed over me in the violet morning light.

"Are you awake?"

Still groggy, I nodded and attempted a smile. I must have looked absolutely ghastly. Somehow I had fallen asleep under the open, starless night sky. I still wore the same clothes as yesterday. Black sand crunched under my hands as I propped myself up.

"Korpusant died during the night. You better leave."

This focused my attention. "Where should I go?"

"Go to the nearest town and lose yourself. That would be Ambreville. If the LAR finds you before then, they will kill you. The LAR will not go into town because they are afraid of the Ambreville Police; of course, they might send an assassin after you."

"They want to kill me?"

"They are, shall we say, unimpressed with your skills as a doctor."

I nodded. No arguing with that. I knew Korpusant would die of his wound. It had only been a matter of time. No one could have saved him, and perhaps I should not have tried. Korpusant's comrades saw my failure as a betrayal, and now I was in big trouble. "What if I went to Combray?" I asked. I had promised myself I would take the urn there. I still meant to keep my word.

"Combray is far beyond Ambreville."

I remembered the dream of Korpusant, and blurted the next question: "What about the Fountain of Youth?"

"That is just a story!" she answered sharply. "No more foolish questions, witch doctor. Get a head start, and leave now!"

"Are you coming with me?" I asked hopefully. She had saved me, and I have to admit, I was a little bit in love with her.

She laughed. "I think not. *Bon voyage!*"

"*Au revoir*," I replied with more optimism than I felt.

"Here," she said, handing me the urn. "This belongs to you. Hurry, before the soldiers wake up. Follow the Way of the Saints to Ambreville."

The Way of the Saints

When I said, 'I saw the way,' this was not what I
meant, not at all. At first, it was not too bad. The
road of glittering black sand out of Bois Caiman was
easy to follow through the jungle. As I progressed,
this road, 'The Way of the Saints,' became little more
than a flat path cleared of vegetation. The terrain
descended almost imperceptibly, and the ground grew
wetter, until I was following less a road, and more a
shallow river of mud. One step after another, I
splashed through standing water and mud flats on the
so-called road to Ambreville. The humidity was
oppressive, as usual, and I sweated copiously. The
gray mud flowed ever so slowly below the over-
arching canopy of purple foliage, and it became
harder and harder to avoid straying from the swampy
path. I was thankful for the thick canopy because it
protected me from the intense sunlight, but it made
navigating by the sun difficult; I knew little about
navigation in the first place, and even less about
where I was going. To make matters worse, I did not

know anything about the sun's movement through the sky. Did it rise in the east? Set in the west? Several times I followed false paths that suddenly ended in a tangle of ferns and gigantic pitcher plants, and I retraced my steps. I concentrated on putting one foot in front of the other, plodding and splashing and cursing, all the while holding on to the urn.

It occurred to me that everything that had happened since last night might be a feverish hallucination induced by the diamond root, a prolonged narcotic dream. Perhaps none of this was real. Was I an unreliable narrator of my own story? I immediately rejected this. Everything around me was absolutely and uncomfortably real.

My foot caught a submerged root, and I stumbled, face first into the muck. It took a lot of effort to get back on my feet. I was hungry and thirsty and too tired to even wipe the mud from my face and shirt. My khaki shirt and cargo pants were covered in the mud of Nouveau Haitiah; nevertheless, I persisted and endured, and I slogged onwards, and so made my way down the watery road to Ambreville.

My pace was slow, and I knew it, but I could not help it. I was a little overweight and definitely out of shape, and woefully unprepared for the demands of this trek. It was too hot. It was too humid. I did not want to be there. For two days and nights I continued without stopping and without sleep, because falling asleep on wet ground in Nouveau Haitiah was the worst thing a person could do. I had heard the stories about annies- parasitic annelids- back at camp. From time to time I glanced backwards, looking for signs of disturbances in the mud, such as bubbles or a roiling action. Remy told me about an old chief named Harado who used annies for executions. The victim would be tied down in the mud. Eventually, the worms found their prey. According to the corpulent orderly, the worms first disabled the arms and legs, leaving the victim conscious, but utterly helpless. Remy's description of the end preyed on my mind.

I briefly considered deviating from the path and making my way through the jungle, and quickly dismissed the idea. The LAR might track me. The annies would also track me if they caught my trail, and movement through the bush would be even slower than following the soggy path. There was no one to turn to, no going back, and no deviating from this road, so I continued, mechanically placing one foot in front of the other, practically asleep on my feet. Just when I thought it could not get any worse, a cloud of arachnoflies found me. The metallic red creatures buzzed about my head and neck, seeking tender exposed skin. Their bites raised painful welts, and no amount of waving and shooing and slapping could keep them away.

Ohm's moss hung in blue-green strands from the purple and yellow cycads. It cut off my line of sight, so I could not see anything in the distance; then again, it made it hard for anyone- or anything- to see me.

As I slogged along the Way of the Saints, I noticed a conical nest near the top of a tall cycad. The nest was fashioned from interwoven branches and ohm's moss, and it steadily dripped water into a small waterhole at the base of the tree. As I paused to watch, a small, shimmering, opalescent blue mock hummer- it looked like a hummingbird, but with four wings and four legs- dove from the nest into the waterhole, splashing headfirst. Moments later, it emerged with a small pale krayfish impaled upon its beak. The wet hummer carried the speared prey straight up to its nest overhead, and disappeared into the nest's dark confines.

The flora and fauna of Nouveau Haitiah, including the mock hummer and krayfish, were interdependent parts of a parasitic process. The same was true for all the flora and fauna of Nouveau Haitiah: much was unseen, and certainly not well understood, whether submerged beneath a pond or river, or hidden high overhead in a dripping nest. Everything seemed connected, and at the same time, its meaning seemed to be concealed in realms beyond my reach, like the ashes of the burned book hidden in the urn's darkness, or my memories before crawling from the pool.

These parasites needed each other in order to reproduce. I understood that. In a sense, all Nouveau Haitian life was just versions of the same thing. The countless varieties of plants and animals pursued one another, seduced one another, and even inflicted suffering on one another, all in order to regenerate; this intermingling was the continuation of the life cycle; in a way it was the highest expression of love.

At that moment, an arachnofly bit me on the crown of my head, and it like being clobbered with a sharp rock. So much for the highest expression of love.

Meanwhile, the urn seemed to grow heavier as I progressed. If I threw it into the bush, no one would know. No one would ever find it. I hefted the urn in one hand, gauging its weight. LAR colors, I noticed once again. Seeing those colors reminded me of the soldiers who had died under my care. Later, I found out the bodies of L'Overture, Toussaint, and Korpusant had been cremated. I was not even carrying the ashes of a body in this urn. Was following through with this commitment to myself worthwhile?

As much as I was tempted, I decided not to throw the urn into the jungle. I had made myself a promise. This urn connected me to the pool, and even though my name had been painted over with LAR colors, it was mine, and I would fulfill this quest. I would take the urn to Combray; but first, I would have to survive long enough to make it to Ambreville, and then avoid anyone from the LAR or Children's Fund.

In the meantime, the Way was becoming drier and more defined. The town must be close. Small, colorful shrines appeared along the roadside, decorated with magenta, yellow, and orange ribbons, as well as crude drawings of people. These were memento mori displays memorializing the dearly departed. The bodies were not actually buried here, of course; the ground was too wet and marshy. Cremation was practiced for good reason. The memento mori shrines did not invoke any memories for me, of course, but they did serve a useful purpose by making the Way easier to follow. That was no small thing, considering my exhaustion and dehydration. Step by step, I knew I was growing nearer, and soon, a primitive, weathered wooden palisade loomed before me. I had come into close contact with the fundamental nature of Nouveau Haitiah, and now, I braced myself to come into close contact with its inhabitants. I rapped upon the faded gate of Ambreville.

AMBREVILLE

I found the cenotaph at the crossroad in the precise center of town. Its inscription read:

"Lest we forget"

The tall black obelisk stood in Ambreville's Plaza de l'Exposition Coloniale, at the main intersection of Macandal and 8th, outside the imposing structure of Government House. I asked a few people about the cenotaph, but no one knew why it had been built, or when, or what event it commemorated, although the carved spears and machetes indicated it was a war memorial. Long lists of names were etched in small writing on each of the cenotaph's eight facets, but the names had been eroded into illegibility by humidity and temperature and time. It did not matter, since most people could not read anyway. The memory- the past- had been betrayed, just as my own past had been betrayed when someone painted over my name on the urn.

Step by step and still carrying it, I passed the black obelisk and walked down the wooden boardwalk of Rue Macandal, dodging passers-by, and stepping over the prone bodies of the poor, the crippled, the inebriated, and the addled. For all I knew, the bodies on the boardwalk could be corpses. Below the boardwalk, at ground level, traffic traversed the dark sandy surface. There were no motorized vehicles, which came as no surprise to me, since there was virtually no metal on Nouveau Haitiah; instead, humans served as beasts of burden, using carts and rickshaws to pull passengers, food, and other goods along the thoroughfare.

The stench of Ambreville pervaded the wooden boards and planks of every building. The jungle's pervasive and somewhat pleasant odor of diamond root, a combination of anise and old campfire, had been supplanted by the city's very human, very unpleasant odors. A combination of low elevation, standing water, and lack of an adequate sewage system resulted in a reek that stunned the senses. The filthy smell coated the corners and hidden places along the elevated boardwalk, and curled around low shanties and other ramshackle structures. It suffused the bright blue and green jury-rigged cloths covering the stalls of vendors and seers at their fortune telling tables, and it even worked its way into the clothing of the crowd. Businessman waved away the arachnoflies and hurried to make their next deal. Apparently the amber trade was centered in Ambreville, and controlled by the Joule syndicate. Shoppers, mostly female, held vanilla perfumed kerchiefs to their noses to mask the odor, while others draped cloth meshes from their wide-brimmed hats. The kerchiefs and veils had the added benefit of protecting them from a contagion they called 'La Fièvre Pourpre.'

I still wore the same muddy clothes, so most of the women gave me a wide birth, with one notable exception. At one point I halted and rested on a bench. An attractive woman in a red-checked dress and without head covering passed close to me. Our glances met. She had remarkable blue eyes and a direct gaze, and much to my amazement, she slowed to a stop.

"Are you lost?" she asked. She looked me up and down. I am sure I did not impress her, but my muddy khaki pants and canvas shirt marked me as an obvious out-of-towner.

"Yes," I answered, "I need help."

"I can help you a little," she said. Without my asking, she gave me a token for a lime, red beans, and rice meal at a nearby vendor.

"*Merci*. I am looking for a place- Combray."

"I have never heard of it."

We went our separate ways. I purchased the food and ate quickly, marveling at her kindness even while shooing away arachnoflies and other airborne arachnids. That was the first time I had ever received charity. I am embarrassed to admit that I could not remember a time when I gave to others in need. Yet she gave freely, with no expectation of getting anything in return. I did not deserve it. How could I ever repay her? I could not; nevertheless, I took that token. I took it gladly, and I relished the food, and I wondered: why did she stop in the first place? Upon reflection, it occurred to me that she must have seen the urn. Perhaps she surmised I was taking it on a pilgrimage to scatter the ashes. While eating, I noticed a sign over a nearby veranda. The sign was unusual for two reasons: first, it had written words on it; and second, it showed a map of Ambreville and surrounding towns. The sign was for an attorney, and advertised that he served clients in Ambreville, Auteuil, and Combray, along with several other places I did not recognize. I finished my meal, walked to the veranda of the lawyer's house, and rapped on the door.

THE LAWYER

"Who are you?" he asked. The lawyer, Burnette, sat behind a large desk. He wore a grey jacket, purple tie, crisp white shirt, and pressed grey slacks.

I stood before him wearing muddy khaki pants and a canvas shirt, and holding the urn. At least my shoes were of good quality, although they were muddy too. I introduced myself.

He ran a pale manicured hand through his neatly groomed silver hair and spoke in a calm, understated tone, the tone of the consummate professional. "Why are you here?"

"I am taking this"- I lifted the urn- "to Combray to scatter the ashes."

"Combray? It is far away." He sat back in his chair and tented his fingers. "What do you need me for?"

"Your knowledge. Your sign shows you can write and you know maps. I am hoping you can help me get there."

"I see." He eyed the urn with undisguised interest. "So you need information?"

"*Oui.* I also need a place to clean up and sleep tonight."

He smirked. "I can see that. You should know I expect compensation up front."

"I have no money."

"Then what can you offer me in return?"

"Information about the LAR?"

"Not interested."

"The Children's Fund?"

He raised his eyebrows. "Is that so? The Fund and I share a long history." He frowned and patted his hands together. "They killed my father in the central square of Combray. Tell me what you know."

I told Burnette about the Children's Fund ambush, its approximate location, the wounds inflicted by the barefoot witch Odette and Chief Harado, and the rumors about Commissar Ampere. Without going into detail, I also mentioned my need to avoid the LAR.

When I finished, he clasped his hands and stared at them for a few moments.

"Chief Harado," he said, narrowing his eyes.

"I saw the fatal wound. It was horrific. The Chief carved an 'H' shaped wound in Toussant's stomach."

He nodded grimly. "That sounds like Harado." He stared at the ceiling for a moment. "There is no way he will ever come to Ambreville. He fears the police." He pursed his lips and nodded, apparently coming to a decision.

"Very well," he said, straightening in his chair. "I will help you and provide some provisions. Go to Auteuil. It is a small town, very remote, about halfway to Combray. You can rest there. The next town beyond it is Combray. It is easy to find. Follow the Way of the Saints. You will reach Auteuil in two to three days. Continue another two or three days from there with your urn, and then you can scatter the ashes in Combray."

"*Merci.* I will."

"You are welcome. You may clean up and then sleep on the sofa in the den. There is a small shrine in the corner with the usual sphere, mirror, and amber die. Use it if you wish." I gave a slight shake of my head, indicating that would not be necessary. He smiled as if we were sharing a secret, and continued. "I will put the urn in a safe place for the night, and return it to you in the morning. Also, you will need a weapon, and you will need an inoculation." He opened a desk drawer and withdrew a black diamond machete in a scabbard. "Here," he said, handing it to me. "My gift to you. In return, you must come back here and inform me about goings-on in Auteuil and Combray, anything you discover about the Children's Fund, and return the weapon at that time."

"I really do not know how to use a machete."

He grimaced. "It is simple. I am sure you will learn."

It was a generous offer, considering I brought so little to the table, but attaching conditions to the machete seemed to undermine the idea of its being a 'gift.' I strapped it to my belt. "What is the inoculation for?"

"La Fièvre Pourpre," he replied. "A case was even reported here in Ambreville. Since I am one of the few people already inoculated, I handled the case personally."

"Are we in danger of an epidemic?"

"No, but the spores are endemic to the region where you are going. The Fever begins with symptoms like asthma, quickly progresses to something similar to pneumonia, then to hemorrhagic fever."

"They are not exactly spores, are they? I thought they were a kind of viral phage," I corrected him. He agreed. He seemed to know something about medicine, and I did not want to reveal my own lack of medical knowledge, so I let the matter rest. We took care of the inoculation, and I prepared to retire to the couch in the next room, but I could not resist asking the lawyer one more question.

"I keep hearing strange rumors about a Fountain of Youth. Do you think there is such a thing?"

"No," he said. And that was the end of the matter, as far as he was concerned.

The next morning, Burnette returned from the boardwalk with breakfast, which he shared with me. He warned me several LAR soldiers were sighted at a vendor on the boardwalk. He did not know if they were looking for me, but they were spreading a strange story about the resurrection of a man named Korpusant. I did not wait around to find out if the LAR soldiers knew I was here. I took the urn and machete, packed a meal, gave the lawyer my thanks, and departed for the Way of the Saints and Auteuil.

THE JOURNEY TO AUTEUIL

The memento mori shrines again decorated the Way of the Saints as I left Ambreville. Fewer appeared as I progressed, until finally there were none at all. There were no other signs of humanity, and I never saw anyone the entire time I was on the path. The air was dense with moisture, the trees were covered with ohm's moss, and the Way became wetter after I crossed a major river, the Bimi. I was again covered with sweat and splattered with mud. Parts of the Way were obscured by purple creepers and violet-hued lianas, which meant I had to hack my way through the tangle with my machete. My food was soon gone, and I realized I would have to go a long way without anything to eat.

While resting, I saw the path behind me looked different. The mud was bubbling and roiling, and from time to time I caught a glimpse of dozens of small humps, the carmine backs of small annelids rising and diving back into the muck. The annies had caught my scent in the mud of Nouveau Haitiah, and now they were slowly but surely pursuing. I picked up the urn and redoubled my pace. I left them far behind, but no doubt they would continue to follow.

In my panicked exhaustion I lost track of time. It must have been days. I did not sleep or eat from that point, and I never rested for long, for fear of falling asleep on my feet. The story Remy told me about how Chief Harado used annies to execute helpless prisoners preyed on my imagination. I could not stay in one place for long, and I could not go back, so step by step I splashed my way along the watery road.

AUTEUIL

I do not remember reaching the low gated palisade of the small settlement of Auteuil, or rapping upon it. I must have staggered through the town's single street, between ramshackle huts in disrepair and abandoned windowless one-room houses leaning at crazy angles. The roofs were covered with blue-green mold and the entire settlement smelled musty. Clearly, no one had lived here for a long time. Skirting a broad shallow puddle, I found myself standing before a large, multi-trunked bodhi tree in a small central square. It was encircled by a low, eight-sided wooden platform. A voice called from a nearby building. It was an old man. He waved, and re-entered the one-room shack. I followed, entered the shack, and stood on the hard dirt floor before the old man, who was seated behind an ancient desk. There was a rickety wooden chair facing the desk, and two other empty chairs in the corners, with three wooden pallets positioned against the wooden walls, apparently serving as beds. There were no windows, just the open door for ventilation; as a result, the room was stifling.

"May I sit down? I am exhausted," I said, clutching the sealed urn to my chest.

The old man gestured to the chair facing the desk.

I collapsed into it and placed the urn next to me. Its black diamond on a yellow background was still visible beneath the mud from The Way of the Saints.

Two other men entered, dressed in dirty amber paramilitary uniforms, although not as dirty and caked in mud as mine. They walked behind the old man's battered desk and took seats in opposite corners. All three were elderly. It struck me because, up until now, I had seen very few old people in Nouveau Haitiah. These old men projected a surly yet casual air of hostility and barely restrained violence. All wore the same small emblem on their chests, a stylized fountain. Presumably this meant they were part of a faction, like the LAR. I read the nametags of the guards. The taller wiry one's tag read 'Lieden." The bald one with bad teeth was named 'Singer.' The man behind the desk did not have a name tag, but seemed to be the oldest; indeed, judging from the deep lines on his face, he was one of the oldest men I had ever seen. From his position behind the desk, and the manner in which Singer and Lieden deferred to him, I assumed he was in command. He rocked back and forth on the hind legs of his chair. From one corner, Singer spoke first. "Welcome to Auteuil." He had a surprisingly high voice.

Lieden leaned forward and asked "Who are you?"

I introduced myself.

The old man jutted out his lower lip, but said nothing. He pointed to the urn on the dirt floor and stared at me with rheumy, bloodshot eyes.

"I carry ashes in this. I am going to Combray to scatter them. I wish I could offer you a gift, but I have nothing to offer."

"Tell me," the old man said. "Why do you carry a yellow urn painted with the black diamond of the LAR?"

I shrugged and shook my head.

"Do you know who I am?"

"No."

"I am Chief Harado. Perhaps you have heard of me?"

He saw my eyes widen with fear, and he chuckled to himself. I had been betrayed by the vessel, with its LAR colors. Behind him, Lieden and Singer giggled at my obvious discomfort.

"I am the head of the Children's Fund."

I opened my mouth to speak, but I was so tired and afraid, and the situation so dire, I could not think of what to say to save myself.

"This is Lieden and this is Singer," he continued. "Singer is a connoisseur of degenerates." Lieden laughed. Chief Harado smirked. "That machete would make a nice gift."

Singer tensed, and Lieden stood and put his hand on the hilt of his machete in case I made a move. Mumbling an apology, I removed the sheathed machete from my belt with clumsy, fumbling fingers, and handed it to Harado, hilt first. He grunted approval and tossed it to Lieden, who placed it next to a shrine on the corner shelf and returned to his chair. The shrine held objects I had seen before: a small blue globe with a yellow and purple spot shaped like a comma, a tiny circular mirror, and a pair of small amber dice.

I sat down again, laboring to breathe. Harado looked me over from behind his desk.

"You look tired, boy. Ugh, you're a mess. Look at you. What happened to your clothes?"

"I came here straight from the Way." I self-consciously brushed my hands across the front of my ochre-stained canvas shirt. "I fell. I have not had the chance to rest or clean up." I was too nervous to stop talking. "These arachnofly bites are killing me."

The Chief burst out laughing. "Oh, my poor boy. My poor, poor boy!" Singer and Lieden joined in the laughter. "Look at you!" Harado continued, speaking to the guards. "Look at his shirt! His clothes! His skin!"

I straightened in my chair. "I do not see what is so funny."

They laughed even harder. Harado slapped his knees and waved his gnarled, bony hands. "Didn't they tell you?"

"Tell me what?"

Wiping away a tear while composing himself, Harado muttered "oh my" to himself. "Listen," he said, "the arachnoflies won't bite if you drape some ohm's moss around your neck."

I bit my lip. No one ever told me this.

Another humorous thought seemed to occur to the old man. "I can see you are out of shape. That much is obvious. But why are you so tired?"

"I had to stay ahead of the annies. I walked three days and nights without sleep."

Singer and Lieden guffawed. Harado's eyes twinkled. He leaned forward and put his elbows on the desk, cupping his chin in his hand and savoring the moment. "Why didn't you bring something to sleep on, like a tarp or a hammock, or even sleep in the crook of a tree? As long as you are off the ground, the annies will not bother you."

I shrugged. I was too tired to care.

Harado wiped his nose with the back of his hand. "Ah well. That was funny."

"It was thoughtless. It was cruel. Someone should have told me. I could have died."

"Yes," Harado agreed. "It was cruel, and it was thoughtless, and it was very funny. And yes, you could have died." He coughed. "You know, most men would not have survived. You are stronger than you look." He stared at me for a long moment. "Tell me, what did you do for the LAR? Tell me a story."

I refused. They were toying with me and I knew it. I had no food, no water, no weapon, I was exhausted, and I did not know anything about fighting, never mind how to defend myself; meanwhile, there were three of them, all experienced killers.

Harado could see I was growing tired of this game. "Listen to me. Combray is the main town for the

Children's Fund, but Auteuil is a nice place. Stay here tonight. We will take turns watching over you, Mister LAR. Tomorrow, after you rest in peace, Lieden and Singer and I will scatter those ashes for you."

'*Oh no you won't,*' I thought. I did not know how I would stop this, but exhausted or not, I would find a way.

"What do you think," Harado asked Singer, "is Mister LAR a degenerate?"

Singer shrugged. "I don't know. Hold out your hands, Mister LAR."

I complied, extended my arms, and turned my hands palm up and palm down.

"Look at his hands!" Singer exclaimed. "Not one callous. I'll bet he's never done an honest day of work in his life!"

"Neither have you!" Lieden interjected.

Singer was right, but I felt a need to justify myself, and said by way of explanation: "I like to read."

Singer chortled. "Oh, he's a degenerate all right!"

"Let's celebrate!" Lieden declared, pulling a small purple pouch from his pocket.

"Yes, let's smoke!" Singer produced a black pipe and passed the pouch and pipe to Harado.

"Good idea!" Harado took the pouch and pipe from Singer, and carefully filled the pipe with sparkling purple crystals. He tamped them down into the pipe's bowl and lit it. After inhaling deeply, he poked the pipe aggressively at me. "Ever smoke this?" he asked.

"Yes." I took the pipe- as if I had a choice. The smoke tasted like ashes and anise.

"Diamond root." Harado explained as the smoke filled my lungs. He placed the pouch of crystals on the top of the desk with great care. "You do not really know Nouveau Haitiah until you really know diamond root, because diamond root is the heart of this world. Where it grows, you find black diamonds. The plant grinds the diamonds into black sand."

"It's a mild stimulant," Lieden added, accepting the pipe from me.

"It's a wild hallucinogen!" Singer said in a high pitched cackle.

"I've heard diamond root is what makes Nouveau Haitians crazy," Harado observed.

"I've heard it's the sunlight," Lieden said. "It's too blue."

"No, too purple," Singer countered.

"Too intense," Lieden said.

Harado took the pipe and drew deeply. A spark fell onto his chest. The old man did not even bother to put out the tiny ember, and after making a pinhole burn, it went out. He was sadistically enjoying having me as a captive audience. "The black diamonds," Harado said, "come from the center of Nouveau Haitiah, you know. The center of the planet is made out of black diamonds!" Lieden snorted. Singer waved his hand at the Chief in good-natured disbelief. "No, it's true!" Harado insisted. The planet draws light from the sun and absorbs it into the core's darkness."

The pipe passed back and forth between them, the bowl crackling with each long draw. Lilac-grey smoke filled the small room with the familiar redolence of ashes and anise. I passed on taking additional draws, and the old men did not seem to care. They continued arguing about what made the planet's inhabitants crazy, but I was completely out of my head.

Memories flowed over and through me, both voluntary and involuntary. They rode the smoke, and came unbidden to me through the haze. I remembered crawling on my hands and knees out of a warm pool. I remembered a field of yellow spear grass at twilight, with eight-legged lightning bugs rising above it like miniature flashing blue-white stars, darting and dancing to natural music. I remembered asking Victoria to come with me to Ambreville. I recalled the foul odors of Ambreville's streets. Did I see a Fountain of Youth? I do not remember. I heard disembodied voices.

"Where is everybody?" I asked the voices.

Harado's voice intruded into the fugue. "Gone, dear boy. Gone, gone, gone."

"Gone crazy?"

Harado laughed.

"The rest of the Fund will be here tonight or tomorrow," Lieden said, "including Commissar Ampere."

"Odette too," Singer chimed in.

"Why is it called the Children's Fund?" I asked. "None of you look like children."

Lieden and Singer thought this was hilarious. Harado took it more seriously. "That is a good question. The original Children's Fund came from Last Call, near the headwaters of the Bimi. Everyone from there looked like children. Something happened-"

"A plague," Lieden interrupted.

"Poison," Singer guessed.

"No, I think the mines gave out," Harado said. "Over the years, other recruits came and went. When Auteuil was abandoned, some of them joined the Children's Fund."

"Most went to Ambreville," Lieden declared.

"No, Combray," Singer said.

"Combray?" I asked.

"Combray," Lieden asserted with a knowing air, "is now the heart of the Children's Fund territory."

"Only a few of the original members of the Fund are left- Commissar Ampere, Odette, a couple of others... Have you heard any stories about Odette, the barefoot witch?" Harado asked mischievously.

I shook my head 'no' for several reasons: 1) I did not believe in witches; 2) I did not want to hear rambling gory tales; 3) the diamond root was making it hard for me to string words into understandable sentences; and 4) I could see no way of escaping Auteuil.

Chief Harado plunged into a rambling narrative about Odette, also known as "The Unofficial Hostess of Nouveau Haitiah." I vaguely listened, but could not take my eyes from Harado's face. He must have thought I was eager to hear the tale, because he leaned across the flimsy desk towards me, eyes dilated, liver-spotted hands clutching the desk's edge, rapidly nodding and talking.

"The stories are true," he said, "if any story can be said to be true in the first place." His gaze burned with conviction. He leaned even closer to me. "Do you believe stories can be true?"

"Sure," I replied. I could not stop looking at his facial features. *'Such age,'* I thought, *'such age.'* Was that dust in the old man's wrinkles?

"They wouldn't be stories in the first place if they were actually true," Lieden interrupted.

"A story is just something you pull out of your ass," Singer interjected. He thought this was very witty, and covered his bad stubby teeth with his hand as he chortled.

"Shut up," Harado snapped. "Stories can be true, even if they never happened."

Chastened, Singer solemnly nodded his assent.

Harado took a deep breath and stared at me. "What should we conclude..." he asked, searching for the right words to flesh out his question. He ran the back of his hand across mouth, and licked his lips. "What should we conclude from the way a being behaves in its dying moment?"

Was it a moment of epiphany for the bitter, bloody old man? Or was he merely referring to his violent, sadistic plans for me? *'The mind dreams after the body dies,'* I thought, but before I could say anything, Lieden jumped in with his opinion.

"Nobody wants to die. Everybody fights like hell to avoid it, especially when someone else is killing them."

Harado agreed, and launched into another tale about a child, murder, and the barefoot witch from the Children's Fund, Odette.

It was unspeakably horrible. I do not want to remember that story.

Instead, I concentrated on the old man's features: the deep wrinkles, the droopy nose covered with a network of broken capillaries, yellowed eyes, and a slight palsy in the hands. *So old.* My concentration was broken by Harado's gleeful voice as it completed the horrible anecdote. Lieden and Singer responded with belly laughs.

That was enough for me. I stood and swayed, barely able to keep my balance. "I have to go now. I have to get some sleep." I picked up the urn and held it to my chest. Pausing at the doorway, I asked "Where are my sleeping quarters?"

Harado waved expansively. "Anywhere you like, boy. Think of this as your hometown. You're part of Nouveau Haitiah now!"

Scattering Ashes

Disoriented by diamond root and exhausted by my trek, I stumbled from the hut into the deserted compound of Auteuil. I came upon the shallow muddy puddle. Setting down the urn, I stripped, and rolled around in the mud. I thought it would wash off the muck from the Way of the Saints, but all I managed to do was cover my entire body in the mud of Nouveau Haitiah. What can I say? My judgment was not good because of the diamond root. I was out of my head. I picked up the urn and crossed the flat abandoned compound, leaving my ruined clothes by the puddle. Instead of the usual packed dirt, I noticed a low groundcover cushioned my bare feet. Each step crushed the low, sparkling purple plants, releasing an aromatic smell, the unmistakable scent of diamond root. I returned to the gigantic, multi-trunked bodhi tree, naked, still clasping the urn to my chest. Its low wooden platform was perfect for sleeping. I stood still for a long moment. It was silent, and only the pounding of my own heart filled my ears. I stared at the tree- I stared down at the urn- and impulsively hurled it at the tree, smashing the vessel to pieces. A few ashen clumps fell to the ground with light muffled thumps, along with shards of pottery, but most of the gray-white ashes bloomed in a slowly expanding cloud which enveloped the tree, the platform, and me; it continued expanding beyond the shallow puddle where I had left my clothes in a pile, as well as Harado's shack. It drifted, thinned, and eventually dispersed, but not before engulfing the entire compound of Auteuil. I brushed away some vessel shards from the wooden platform and reclined on it, resting on my right side. Ashes and mud covered me, but I ignored that too, and fell into a deep dreamless sleep.

FEVER

A splash from somewhere nearby woke me. I opened my eyes. The mottled gray bark of one of the bodhi tree's trunks was inches away from my face. I did not know the time, but the quality of the daylight seemed wrong. Sore, disoriented, naked, and famished, I sat up and faced the direction of the splash.

Harado sat in the shallow puddle next to my clothes. He rocked slightly back and forth, hugging himself. I approached, full of dread and a sense of unreality, and he stopped rocking. His scrawny arms were folded and his grizzled chin rested on his chest. He drew a rattling breath and exhaled.

"Chief Harado?"

He did not reply. Thin red trickles ran from the corners of his mouth, nose, and ears. He shivered.

I took another step closer and repeated his name, with no response. Then I shouted "Chief Harado! What is wrong? You are bleeding!"

The old man looked up with bright, unfocused, bloodshot eyes. "Who are you?"

When I reminded him he muttered to himself in an angry tone, and resumed rocking back and forth. He was concealing something in his folded arms.

"Come closer," he said.

I kept my distance.

"You are the carrier," he said.

"I carried the urn. I scattered the ashes yesterday when I broke it."

He nodded. "It was in the ashes." He coughed and began shaking more violently. "La Fiev... ". He coughed until he choked, and then spit blood.

I realized what he was trying to say: 'La Fièvre Pourpre.'

How had the disease come to Auteuil? Why did Harado call me 'the carrier'? Then it dawned on me. The Fever spores must have been in the urn. And that meant the lawyer Burnette must have done this. But why? Burnette knew I had been with the LAR. He thought I was going to scatter the ashes in Combray, in the heart of Children's Fund territory, but instead I scattered them here. Burnette must have been targeting the Fund because they killed his father in Combray. To him, I was just the agent for delivery. At least he had the decency to vaccinate me against the spores; or at least, he told me he did. I felt no ill effects. Yet Burnette must have assumed delivering the urn with its LAR colors would mean my death at the hands of his enemy. The sheer murderousness of his plot left me stunned. He was willing to kill on a scale I had never imagined.

Harado's wheezing brought me back to the moment. He pointed at me with one hand and motioned me closer. He tried to speak again and managed one last word. I think he said "betrayal," but I was not sure. The effort set off another round of coughing. One final, violent fit racked his narrow chest, and slowly subsided. A frothy, pink bubble expanded from his lips and popped. Harado went limp, slumping sideways into the shallow brown water; as he slumped, a long metal object slipped from his folded arms and into the puddle.

It was a machete.

For a moment, I was speechless. He was going to kill me. That was how an intelligent being behaved in the dying moment.

What about the guards, Lieden and Singer?

Still naked, I picked up the machete and quietly crossed the compound to Harado's quarters. The door was open. I cautiously approached, and paused when the wooden threshold creaked under my foot. "Lieden? Singer?" No answer. I looked inside.

They sat in opposite corners of the small shabby office. Neither moved. Singer was sprawled in his chair, head back, arms and legs stiffly extended. His mouth gaped, pulling his lips tight and away from his stubby brown teeth, as if he were laughing at one final macabre joke. Lieden slumped in his seat against the wall's wooden planks. His open sightless eyes seemed to stare at the black pipe and the purple pouch of diamond root still setting on Harado's desk. Like Harado, both Lieden and Singer had dried blood running from their eyes, nose, ears, and mouth. A single metallic blue arachnofly crawled across Lieden's nose.

I left the dilapidated office and returned to sit in the shade of the bodhi tree, with its lovely groundcover of purple diamond root. In the past days I had witnessed old age, disease, suffering, and death, and for the first time, my experiences with them confirmed my own personal ability to persist and prevail. So I was a part of this now. There was no going back. I had fulfilled my quest to scatter the ashes from the vessel. True, Auteuil was not Combray, but Auteuil would have to do. In the meantime, I needed to leave Auteuil as quickly as possible. Commissar Ampere and his daughter, the so-called witch Odette, along with the rest of the Children's Fund could arrive here at any moment. I dressed, and helped myself to a few of the belongings of Harado, Lieder, and Singer, including the sheathed machete originally given to me by Burnette. I also took the pouch of diamond root and pipe, since they might be useful for barter. In another shack I found food, which was very welcome. After a quick meal of red beans, rice, and a lime, I was able to think more clearly. Going back along the Way of the Saints to Ambreville was a bad option. I did not want to run into the LAR or Burnette again. Going to Combray

seemed like an even worse idea, since I now knew
that was the heart of the Children's Fund territory. I
selected a little-used path that ran perpendicular to
the Way of the Saints, and made my way back into the
tangled jungle of Nouveau Haitiah.

THE GRAND MAESTRO

Blame it on books.

When I took that path and arrived at the University, I had nothing but the clothes on my back, a machete, a pocketful of survival items, and a new understanding of my place in the world. Right then, my place in the world did not look good. Understanding and a sense of belonging in my world was a wonderful thing, but I was thirsty and starving. I traded the pipe and pouch of purple crystals for some food, but that did not last long. For months, I stayed alive by scavenging in a dumpster behind a university building.

Students at the university were like students everywhere: immersed in their studies, and poor. They were generous when possible, and usually kind, but generally speaking, they ignored me. Who could blame them? I was a thin, ill-shaven, middle-aged man who always wore the same dirty clothes and slept on a park bench. Perhaps it was out of pity, or perhaps from a fear they would end up like me, but to their credit, the students occasionally provided me with a token or petite madeleine.

Eventually, I struck up a conversation with a student named Armstrong. We discovered a mutual love of books and became friends. He took me in and shared his food and the shelter of his tiny hut. He was shorter than me, with a slight build and a big nose, wiry black hair, and a dark complexion. I read and re-read Armstrong's collection of books, and over the following months my love of literature came to the attention of one of Armstrong's instructors, Professor Alihak. Coincidentally, the Professor was born in Auteuil, but I never brought up what happened to me there. The Professor became my mentor, and less than a year after fleeing Auteuil, I was admitted into the University on a scholarship. That was fortunate, because even though I was a little old to be a student, I had nowhere else to go. I still could remember nothing of my life prior to crawling on my hands and knees from that warm pool, and since then, I wanted to forget everything that had happened, and instead, concentrate on school. My education came to a crescendo with my graduate thesis on the novel by

Marcel Proust, *A La Recherche du Temps Perdu*. I even earned the title of class Valedictorian, which is more than I could say for the unearned title of 'The Doctor' given to me by the LAR.

My thesis described the solace and redemption found in the persistence of memory, achieved through the act of reading. When a work of art was read at some future time, its words brought memories alive within a new context- it resurrected them. Through the combination of memory and the art of writing, a person could be saved and achieve a form of future immortality through reading. It was a comforting thought, to believe life was not meaningless and impermanent. Life could become meaningful because now it lasted, it was permanent, and therefore worthwhile after all. What can I say? Armstrong never really bought it, even though he was much younger than me. He actually laughed at me! However, Professor Alihak was my mentor, and he absolutely loved this stuff.

Alihak was a handsome man. He was tall, thin, charismatic, and graceful as a wading stilt, especially in the way he moved his hands. He dressed well for a person from academia, typically wearing a black suit, white shirt, narrow black tie, and polished black shoes, and although older than most of the other professors, he moved with great energy. His intellect was imposing, but his most memorable asset was his melodic baritone voice.

It was funny how often Alihak and I were mistaken for one another. We looked nothing alike! How could anyone confuse our identities? He was taller than me by several inches, much older, and his voice was deeper. His hands were graceful, while mine were meant to read books. He was my mentor, a writer, and instructor. I was his student and reader.

Armstrong and I played one prank on Alihak that had far-reaching results. One day, Armstrong captured an injured scarlet mock mynah. We kept the strange four-winged, four-legged feathered creature in a cage, and nursed it back to health. It was not a nice creature, and capable of giving nasty scratches with its claws, but Armstrong seemed fond of it.

Since I still remembered Victoria and often thought of her, Armstrong and I decided to teach the creature to sing the word 'Victoria' just for a lark. The mock mynah was a master of mimicry, and our project was a spectacular success. Not only did the mock mynah learn to sing it, but after we released it, the creature taught the other mock mynahs in the wild to sing 'Victoria' as well; soon, the jungles of Nouveau Haitiah reverberated with their one-word song. They did not just sing it, either, but would reproduce the word in different tempos and with unexpected harmonies. The bird-like beasts would improvise, croon, wail, shout, scream, cackle and screech 'Victoria,' competing to see which could produce the most impressive version, or at any rate, the loudest. It made everybody crazy. We spread the rumor that Alihak had trained them. Everyone blamed him for the noisy mock mynahs, and that irritated him to no end. From then on, some referred to him as 'The Grand Maestro,' and oh, how he would scowl if anyone called him that to his face!

But all good things come to an end, and it was eventually time for me to graduate. For Graduation

Day, Alihak was scheduled to give the commencement speech, and as Valedictorian, I was supposed to follow him with a farewell speech on behalf of my class. Coincidentally, 'valedictorian' actually means 'to say farewell.' I never did give that speech; nevertheless, I retained the title. Since then, everything that occurred to me could be seen as one long, continuous process of saying farewell; farewell to my reading; farewell to books; farewell to art; farewell to memories; and farewell to the world immortalized in Proust's work, a world utterly disconnected from my world, the world of Nouveau Haitiah.

GRADUATION DAY

Tick, tock, tick, tock...

The ceramic pendulum of the clock on the classroom wall ticked off the seconds of this last and final course. I closed my book and placed it on the worn, smooth surface of the desk, shifted in the chair that was too small for me, and placed my hands on top of a philosophy textbook resting on the desktop. It contained one of my favorite lines: "I think, therefore I am." I admired that line a great deal. It made a terrific starting point. However, I could never accept the logic beyond that first point; nothing was proven, not for certain, and that left me treading water in a pool of philosophical solipsism. In solipsism- 'self alone,' or 'solo self'- the mind exists, but outside of one's own mind, nothing is certain. Even the external world may not exist.

Books encouraged solipsism because, through the suspension of disbelief, books shut out the world of the senses and replaced them with an alternative, self-contained world, one which did not necessarily correlate with what was real. While books immersed me in a rich interior life, they alienated me from the world outside my window. As it turns out, the external world was unwilling to remain alienated from me. It was Graduation Day, and the external world was about to come crashing through my door.

Roughly one hundred students sat in the main lecture hall, a building which was little more than a large, glorified barn. The hall was surrounded by dilapidated outbuildings which served as classrooms. I sat near the front, next to Armstrong. Outside the tall window next to me, I could see another building constructed of wooden planks faded by the too-intense sun. It stood amid the tall xanthia grass which dominated this region of gently rolling fields, south of Ambreville.

The instructor at the front of the room made the announcement we had all been waiting for. "Ladies and Gentlemen, this concludes the course. Congratulations! And now, I would like to introduce the next speaker, Professor Alihak." She collected textbooks on her way to the back of the hall, and exited, quietly closing the large double doors behind her.

Professor Alihak strode to the front of the hall to the cadence of polite applause, projecting his usual air of barely restrained vitality. Carrying a prop in one hand, he ascended the stairs two steps at a time and bounded across the stage, waving and smiling, then took his position behind the podium. He set the prop upon it, a large black sand hourglass. Alihak flipped the hourglass and addressed us. "When the sand runs out, I will stop talking, I promise!" The comment generated some good natured laughter. His classes were popular, and anyone who attended knew his lectures could run on and on, especially when it came to the subject of time. When Alihak gave his Graduation Day speech, my mentor still went by the modest title of 'Professor,' but he had already written his great book, *Redeeming Time and Memory*. Later, he claimed the title 'Alihak, The Grand Maestro, The Only Miracle, and Professor of Popular Education, Science, and Culture.' He was the most brilliant man I had ever known. At times he could be introverted, subdued, and deferential; at other times gregarious, thoughtless, and even cruel, ranting about whatever popped into his head. At this point, as my mentor prepared to deliver his oration, I thought he was merely unstable. I soon came to realize he had gone far beyond 'unstable.' After a few more introductory remarks he began his speech.

"How long will we endure?" he asked. "How long will we persist? Will we last as long as the black diamonds of Nouveau Haitiah? They endure, even as they are ground into granular crystals by the diamond root plant; afterwards, they continue to persist in the form of black sand," he said, patting the top of the hourglass. "If each of us is ground down to a grain of sand, then how long will we endure, my students? How long will we persist?"

Alihak spoke in a deep, mellifluous bass, illustrating his words with graceful gestures, raising and lowering his voice while varying the tempo. Although Armstrong and I had heard versions of this speech before, the hypnotic effect of Alihak's voice was difficult to resist. The rest of the students stirred in their seats and exchanged questioning glances. This was supposed to be a commencement speech, but the Professor seemed to be heading in an odd direction.

"Diamond root grows low to the ground," he continued. "It never grows tall, but it spreads far and wide. It spreads horizontally, seeking black diamond deposits beneath our low jungle canopies, transforming them into vast black sandy dunes and beaches. As a result, the land itself has become low and flat too. We have no mountains worth mentioning. There is little difference between the elevation of the land and the surrounding sea. And the continent itself is circular in shape. Topography is truth. Geography is fate. Even the ecology is circular; indeed, the same genetic structure that pervades diamond root pervades this entire ecology of parasitic mutualism."

Tick, tock, tick, tock...

"How did we get here? Were we banished to this place? Did someone send us here, and then forgot? Who knows? I suppose that is the result of smoking too much diamond root!"

The students responded with an appreciative yet uneasy laugh. I sat back in my wooden chair, extended my legs, and examined my fingernails, repeating that old line to myself: 'these hands were meant to read books.' Meanwhile, Alihak's words seemed to float out the window and lose themselves in the tall yellow fields of swaying xanthia grass. The whispering stalks called to me in return, a wordless invitation to give up the life of the mind, and join the timeless alien landscape.

Tick, tock, tick, tock...

"Oh, my students! Today is Graduation Day. For many of you, today ends your formal education. Time is up. Have you found salvation through education? No? That is a pity. How can you be saved if you have no more time?" He smiled and took in the hall with his gaze.

"There is an answer. There is a new kind of salvation that comes to you through this world. It comes to you through me."

This caught my attention.

"Traditionally, religious salvation has a vertical orientation. It is like climbing the rungs of a ladder, or progressing through the grades of school. It involves climbing and ascension, because the idea is to escape the confines of this world and achieve a higher, different one; in other words, to graduate."

A metallic red arachnofly flew through the open window and buzzed over my head. It performed a couple lazy loops, its buzz rising and falling in time with the words of the Grand Maestro.

"The ecology of Nouveau Haitiah offers a glimpse of a new kind of salvation. It offers immortality through reincarnation, through a natural process of recycling. This reintegration relies upon a horizontal orientation, not vertical; instead of climbing a series of rungs like a ladder, it is like being immersed in a round pond.

"This natural Nouveau Haitian text is also writ large upon the heavens. We hear it in the music of the spheres," he said, raising both arms as if preparing to cue an orchestra, "and I am the conductor. We orbit the sun in an almost perfect circle, which means there is little difference between seasons. Our years run together in a continuum, a cycle, without beginning and without end.

"But what is salvation? And what is time?" He paused and thumped the top of the hourglass, and then raised his eyebrows up and down in a mischievous manner, and left the stage. The Professor bounded over to the ceramic clock on the wall, scratched his head, and then moved his fingers around the dial, as if adjusting the hour hand. He threw his hands in the air in frustration and made an exaggerated sign of the crossroads gesture, and then returned to the podium to resume his rambling speech.

"The traditional view depicts time in a linear sequential passage, an orderly procession from beginning to end, from admission to graduation. But if you truly become a part of Nouveau Haitiah, then everything is different! There is no birth, no immaculate conception, no rise and fall into corruption, no meaningless death; instead, there is recycling, an immersion and integration into an ongoing continuum. It is a karmic wheel of cause and effect, spinning like mad, until cause and effect become one, and there is only simultaneity. That is salvation. *That* is the true nature of time.

"Trapped within this circular flatness we endure, and we persist, like arachnoflies trapped in amber, waiting for the shock of integration. Let us abandon the old ways and become fully integrated into our world, our globe, our Nouveau Haitiah. We must embrace our evolutionary convergence with our world's parasitic ecology, for this flat circularity is also our vanity mirror."

I laughed to myself at the mention of 'amber' and 'the shock of integration.' The etymological root of 'electricity' was *electricus*, which meant 'of amber.' The objects on most Nouveau Haitian shrines were a small globe, mirror, and amber dice, with amber's electricity as the animating element. Not surprisingly, the amber dice also represented chance and fate. As for the globe, it represented the usual symbolism associated with a sphere, and the mirror connoted vanity and illusion, as well as a pond.

"You! Yes, you! You are part of this too! We seek affirmation. We seek redemption. Will you consider our plight? Here we are in Nouveau Haitiah, trapped like characters within the flat pages of an unopened novel- say, *Redeeming Time and Memory*." He tilted his head and wagged a finger. "I am pretty sure some of you never did open it, even though it was assigned reading. I am looking at you, Armstrong!" The students chuckled, and Armstrong, one of Alihak's favorites, laughed loudest of all.

"In any case," Alihak continued, "we are like characters trapped in an unopened novel; we are ignored by humanity, and then lost, and then utterly forgotten. When that happens, my words are just unuttered sounds. The letters of the alphabet are just signs without significance. The words and sounds only contain the meaning you give them as you read. So what do most of you do? You imagine yourselves at a safe distance, removed by arm's length from the book in your hands, and you treat this reading experience like a tourist; you casually assign meaning and context, and think you are uninvolved."

Outside, I could hear a scarlet mock mynah wailing her name:

Vic-tooooor-ia

"And yet," Alihak continued, "you cannot help but be involved. You are involved right now! I am called The Only Miracle for good reason, and it is NOT for teaching those mock mynahs to sing 'Victoria'! It wasn't me, I swear!"

We all enjoyed another laugh. Alihak smiled, held up one graceful hand, and resumed.

"Some of you ask me why I wrote *Redeeming Time and Memory.* I did it to capture memory and make it immortal- or at any rate, undying- through art. It is a kind of redemption. But no matter how much detail I provided and no matter how many volumes I wrote, my memories could not be set down in their entirety, exactly as they actually occurred. Thanks to you students- and thanks to you, readers- the memories I recorded will come alive again in the future in a new context, within the setting of your imaginations. The words take on a life of their own. They circumscribe their own reality. Once read, they cannot be 'unread,' although some of you have given it your best shot- I have seen the way some of you sleep at your desks. I am impressed! Nevertheless, you cannot banish them by closing the book or sleeping; in other words, you cannot banish me. And that is why I write.

"I see by the looks on some of your faces that you do not believe this." He nodded and paused for a moment of self-reflection, and then smiled to himself.

"Perhaps you will not listen to my commencement speech. Perhaps you will put down your books, stop reading, and see this as the end of your education. All right, then. Ask yourself this: what is the difference between a page you read in a book, and my world of Nouveau Haitiah? The difference is for that for you, books involve a suspension of disbelief. It is only a suspension and it is temporary. You never truly believe it.

"For me, Nouveau Haitiah is quite real.

"Perhaps you will take a pause from your reading, and glance out the window, and see tall trees or a lake or a street or some random thing. If *I* look out *your* window, oh my students, I will see yellow xanthia grass swaying in the breeze. Remember, Nouveau Haitiah is circular and isolated and self-contained. Even the word 'Haitiah' is a palindrome, circling back upon itself. For me, Nouveau Haitiah is quite real. Nouveau Haitiah has always existed. It will always exist. You may think it can be circumscribed by the walls of a lecture hall or by closing the book cover. Closing the cover may make me an expatriate, but I tell you, I will break through my exile and speak. You, my students, will free me through your post-graduate studies, and I love you for it."

The room was stifling hot, and we were all anxious for the conclusion. The hourglass was nearly empty. Everyone could see his commencement speech was near an end, and the moment of graduation was at hand. We were excited, and Alihak was playing to us. Beads of sweat covered his forehead as he weaved and swayed in time with his worlds. Like a conductor leading an orchestra, his large hands glided like graceful birds, illustrating his meaning. His sonorous tone slowly rose in pitch and intensity, and the tempo increased, as the long crescendo built to a climax. The students began to clap and cheer. A few rose from their seats in anticipation of the end and the moment of graduation. Alihak leaned towards them, grasping the podium and shouting over their whoops and yells and roars of approval.

"You, oh my students, will be my future liberators through the act of reading. Even after I am long gone, I will speak to you from beyond the grave. You will be my saviors and redeem me. I will continue speaking long after this commencement speech ends. I will endure and persist long after you put the books down. It can't be helped.

 "We all endure. We all persist. Ultimately, we do so for one reason. We persist long enough to prevail- prevail in love."

A loud, nearly simultaneous double bang at the back of the room obscured those words for most of the people in the hall. I heard them because I was sitting in front. Professor Alihak frowned and peered at the back entrance, eyebrows knit in irritation over the interruption. Armstrong and I turned in our chairs and looked towards the rear to see what caused the noise.

The double doors at the back of the room had been flung open, and the silhouette of a large man filled the entryway. "Time's up!" He leaned over and rolled an object down the hall's center aisle, towards Professor Alihak. As it rolled past me, I realized it was a ceramic grenade, and its fuse was burning.

Alihak crouched behind the podium. Pandemonium erupted in the hall. I jumped from my chair, took a giant step, and leaped head first through the open window, arms stretched before me as if I were leaping into a pool. I hit the bare ground, rolled, and stood. Armstrong followed. As he came through the window, the grenade detonated in a flash of orange flame and light. The blast's pressure propelled him farther than me, and he landed hard on his stomach. A piece of debris landed near his feet. It was the clock pendulum. To my amazement, Alihak climbed out the ruined window and stumbled towards us, feebly slapping at a smoldering ember on his black suit, now marred with gray ash and bits of paper. Thin trickles of blood ran from his ears and nose.

Near the entrance, a group of soldiers wearing amber paramilitary uniforms stood in a knot around their standard bearer, casually brandishing machetes. They were waiting for students to flee. Armstrong jumped to his feet and ran towards the soldiers. I recognized the flag carried by the standard bearer. It was saffron with a stylized blue fountain on its field. It was the Children's Fund!

"Armstrong, stop!" I was too late.

Why did Armstrong run towards the soldiers? I think he just panicked, but I will never know for sure. One of them took a few steps towards Armstrong, and with one swing of the machete, he killed him. And that was it for my best friend and one of the kindest people I had ever met. One moment he was here- the next, gone.

Students staggered from the lecture hall, which was now on fire, pursued and killed on the spot by the Children's Fund fighters. Other small buildings, barns and sheds also came under attack. A redheaded woman of middle age ran from the nearest building, the Center for Studies of Nouveau Haitian Flora, followed by a man of similar age. I recognized her. It was Professor Koppes and her husband. She was the top naturalist on Nouveau Haitiah. I took her classes. I think she was the most rational person I have ever met. Before the couple could make it to the safety of the tall xanthia grass, a fighter ran them down. The unarmed husband turned to face the soldier while she kept running. He never stood a chance; the soldier took him down with a machete; however, he clung to the soldier's leg with his dying strength, giving Professor Koppes enough time to make it to the safety of the field, and disappear among the tall yellow grass.

So far, none of the fighters had paid attention to Alihak and me. One of them knelt by the body of Armstrong.

"Come on!" I exclaimed.

"What?" Alihak shouted, cupping his ear. "I can't hear anything. What did you say?"

The blast must have deafened him. I grabbed his arm and dragged him towards the cover of the tall xanthia grass.

"Wait!" Alihak said. "We must help them! We must take a stand!"

"There is nothing we can do," I said.

Alihak wiped blood from his upper lip. "My ears are ringing. I can barely hear you."

A soldier pointed at us and yelled to his comrades.

"Run!"

The soldier ran after us. Another student with his clothes on fire staggered out of the building directly into the fighter's path. The fighter stopped to cut him down.

"Keep running!" I pulled Alihak by the elbow after me, into the yellow xanthia grass.

"Can't we save anyone?" he asked in a tight voice.

"No," I replied. "Not today. If we put some space between us and the University, we might be able to save ourselves."

I led, pushing through the high stalks, and the grass quickly enveloped us in its rancid odor.

Alihak jerked his arm from mine. "We have to do something." We stopped and faced one another. He stood tall, breathing hard, with his arms at his sides and his hands clenched into fists. He surprised me when his entire body jerked, as if he were having a fit. It passed as quickly as it started. His eyes gleamed. "Let's kill them."

"What?" I shook my head in disbelief. We were both unarmed; not only that, we were both academics, and knew nothing about fighting. "Forget it. I know what to do." He seethed as I pulled him deeper into the seemingly endless sea of tall yellow grass, until at last we lost ourselves amid the alien flora.

105

THE ROAD TO LUTETIA HOSPITAL

Alihak was hurt worse than I thought. His ears were
bleeding, so he may have burst his eardrums, but I
could not tell for sure, and I was worried the
concussive force of the grenade may have scrambled
his brain. My nearly non-existent medical skills were
no match for this. I decided we should skirt the town
of Piezo and go to the nearest hospital at Lutetia,
away from both Illiers and Combray and Children's
Fund territory.

The xanthia grass gave way to snake grass, which was
a problem. The low, scaled, metallic gray grass waved
to and fro in slow motion, as if one organism. This
vast patch was preying upon the xanthia grass, and we
had to detour around it. Snake grass was only ankle
high, but each blade could give a painful nip, and even
though it could not break the skin, walking through it
was not a good option. Eventually, the snake grass
gave way to a broad, encroaching field of spear grass,
which preyed upon the snake grass in turn; the spear
grass attacked underground, using its root system to

parasitize the snake grass, in order to reproduce. Alihak and I discussed this.

"Isn't it amazing?" Alihak asked, spreading his arms wide as if to encompass the world. "So much happens in realms we cannot even see: underground, underwater, on a microbial basis, and on scales so large we cannot even perceive them."

"Everything is eating each other," I said. "The world is consuming itself."

"It will go on with or without us," he observed, and suddenly turned manic with enthusiasm. "What a remarkable cycle! How wonderful! How very, very wonderful!"

His enthusiasm irritated me. "Wonderful? It seems like a lot of unnecessary pain and suffering."

"Don't be so grim," Alihak said. "There is a kind of beauty in it. The world's molecular matter constantly re-arranges its configuration. It is a constant act of creation: xanthia grass, snake grass, spear grass... This is creative destruction! The world's life dies- the world's life lives- and dies- and lives. Yes, forms change, of course. Shapes change. Yet through birth, death, and rebirth, energy persists." He gazed into the distance, and then focused on me, and smiled. "Do you see the unity?"

I did not, and told him so.

After a long silence I spoke again. "If an individual's memory does not persist, there is no unity and there is no solace."

It got worse. We crossed a field of straw yellow spear grass and resumed walking upon the dusty road. Later, we stopped for a rest. I sat on a boulder next to the Grand Maestro. He was sitting on the ground, busily scribbling with one finger in the dust.

"What are you doing?" I asked politely.

"Writing a book."

This raised my eyebrows. "I don't see any paper."

He took a deep breath. "The ground is real. It is the body of the world. It persists. Memory persists through writing and reading, so I am writing on the ground. You, of all people, should understand."

That was alarming. It made no sense, and for a moment I was at a loss for words. Was Alihak losing his mind? He continued tracing letters in the dust. After an awkward silence, I decided to play along, and I asked an obvious question. "What are you writing about?"

He grunted. "Animating zombies; instead of creating fictional characters for my novels, I want to make them alive, and real. I want to create real characters in this real world."

"What! Wait a minute. That makes no sense. Zombies are not real. Zombies and a novel's characters are completely different things."

"How would *you* know?"

"You are being weird on purpose. Knock it off."

Alihak stared at me for a long moment, and then nodded once. "Suppose I wrote about you after you died?"

"Suppose you did?"

"Would that make you feel better?" he asked reasonably. "If someone read about you and remembered you, would that cheer you up?"

"Oh, for crying out loud! That would not do me any good at all," I answered. "That would just be a character, not me, doing your bidding and walking through a made-up plot like one of your so-called zombies. I am not a device for you or anyone else. Just because someone else has a memory of me does not mean I exist. There is no truth after death- not for me. Becoming part of someone else's story doesn't even qualify as a consolation prize." I took a deep breath and reconsidered. "Of course, it would be worse to be forgotten altogether."

Alihak laughed at me and shook his head self-indulgently. "You are *so* gloomy." He resumed writing in the dust.

After another march on the road to Lutetia, we paused by a broad shallow lake. The old man was having a tough time. I could tell he was damaged. He no longer walked with his characteristic energy and vigor. Sometimes he shuffled and fell behind. A possible concussion was not the only problem; he must have been depressed about the destruction of his beloved University. I know I was. I often thought of my friend Armstrong.

Alihak abruptly sat down in the damp soil. His hands shook and twitched.

"Professor, are you all right?" I asked. Despite the wetness, I sat on the ground next to him and held both of his hands in mine, hoping it would calm him.

"*Oui*," he replied. His hands continued to quiver. He was oblivious to my attempts to calm him.

"Are you sure? Your eyes are dilated. There is dried blood on your ear lobe."

"I am fine." He pulled his hands free from mine, stood as abruptly as he had sat earlier, and resumed walking towards Lutetia Hospital without even looking back at me. As we walked, he quickened his gait and strode ahead of me, humming aimlessly. Clearly he was not doing well. He needed treatment as soon as possible.

It was hot and dry. How I wish we carried canteens! I caught up with him and he quit the aimless humming.

We walked for a while in companionable silence. Eventually I attempted to engage him in conversation, and posed a question I thought my former mentor would not be able to resist. "If a building burns down," I asked, picturing the lecture hall on Graduation Day, "and I am the only one who remembers it, does the building still exist?"

He rolled his eyes in exasperation. "No."

"If I am the only one who remembers, did it *ever* exist?"

Alihak gave me a withering stare. "You know, it is not always all about you." At first I was taken aback, and then his response angered me, so I left him behind while trotting ahead to reconnoiter.

Although I quickly got over my anger, it would take a long time to for me understand why his answer was both appropriate and wise. Really, I should have understood right then and there, considering my fascination with solipsism. Now I have only regrets. It would be the last time we had a one-on-one conversation. Running ahead to reconnoiter provided me yet another opportunity to play the part of

Valedictorian, and say farewell to the man I left behind me, my brilliant mentor; ah, if only I had known what the next roll of the amber dice would bring!

We fell in with a handful of University refugees, and they agreed to accompany us to Lutetia Hospital. We hoped there would be safety in numbers- at least, that was the theory- but none of us were armed. Alihak and I had no provisions, so we were fortunate that they had some food to share- pink beans, rice, and a large bag of candied ginger. I asked them if they knew what had happened Professor Koppes after the attack on the University; the last time I saw her, she was fleeing into the xanthia grass. No one knew.

In one of his rare lucid periods, Alihak demanded we occupy the hospital and make it into a base of operations. Exactly what kind of operations a bunch of unarmed university students were supposed to conduct escaped me, but then, strategic thinking had never been the Professor's strong suit.

The hospital itself sat upon a low hill, with a broad lawn leading up to its whitewashed façade. The rear backed onto jungle. The building was nearly deserted; the few remaining staff had seen us coming and fled. They must have thought we were a fighting faction, but we were really nothing more than a bunch of refugees. We should have pursued them and persuaded them to join us, or at least convinced them to stay on the grounds. If nothing else, they might have been able to treat Alihak.

We occupied the hospital and set up housekeeping, but that did not last long. It turns out the staff fled because they thought we were mercenaries for the JS, the Joule Syndicate. Apparently they had been spotted in the area, looting and pillaging. Occupying the hospital turned out to be a deadly mistake, because the mercenaries soon found us.

The Joule Syndicate was all about money and amber. We possessed neither. Without hospital staff on the premises to offer as hostages, we had nothing of value. University students did not count. The mercenaries gathered upon the front lawn and prepared to attack. Professor Alihak, the Grand Maestro, the Only Miracle, chose that moment to mount a second story balcony overlooking the lawn and make an incendiary speech.

First, he introduced himself: "I am Alihak, The Grand Maestro, The Only Miracle, and Professor of Popular Education, Science, and Culture." It rapidly went downhill from there. With a gleam in his eye- the same as when he said 'let's kill them' after the attack on the University- Alihak dared the JS troops to come after us inside our 'base of operations' and assured them we would kill them all if they did. He went on to say he knew The Doctor in charge of the resurrection at Bois Caiman, and that Doctor was a charlatan. He declared he was a real witch doctor who would reanimate them after they died and turn them into zombies, and, just to top it off, made fun of their poverty, insulted their mothers, and challenged their manhood. I went upstairs to drag him away from the balcony. It gave me my first chance to see the JS mercenaries.

They looked more like a filthy mob than a faction. Most wore tattered business clothes, torn shirts, and dirty slacks, and many carried machetes. This really

was an impoverished lot, even by Nouveau Haitiah's
standards. Joule was probably not paying them much.
Why should he? Joule did not even bother to go into
the field because he was too overweight to leave
town, and too rich to bother personally pillaging for
trinkets; in turn, the mercenaries would not go into
any town because they would be shunned. The JS flag
reflected their poverty. It was a simple affair, a dark
amber field with a white lightning bolt, and the
soldiers milled around it. When the ragtag mob saw
me on the balcony, they mistook me for Alihak. They
swore and jeered at me, shook their fists, and
immediately launched an attack against the main
entrance.

My fellow students barricaded the main doors, but the
mercenaries quickly broke them down and charged
into the lobby. Most of the students died right there.
I heard their groans and screams and pleas, but I am
ashamed to say that even though I knew some of
them well- their names, their likes and dislikes, their
hopes and dreams and so on- I ignored them. I heard
them begging for life, and I ignored them and hid near
the second floor balcony. That is the truth. I was

trying to survive and I was trying to save Alihak and I was unarmed. The situation was dire and I was in over my head.

Eventually the screams and crying stopped. I waited a long time, hoping the JS troops would leave. Fortunately, Alihak cooperated with me by remaining silent. The Professor and I quietly descended from the balcony to the first floor lobby, hoping to sneak out the front. As we neared the bottom of the staircase we were spotted by two soldiers.

One was a middle-aged soldier with greasy slicked back hair, medium height, wearing a businessman's garb consisting of a dark blue shirt with a soiled white collar, red tie, mustard yellow suspenders, and stained slacks. The businessman shouted "Hey Buddy!" and went after Alihak, waving his machete. Alihak fled up the stairs, while I jumped over the banister and dropped a short distance to the ground floor. I landed without hurting myself and raced down a hall. Behind me I heard a cry, followed by a triumphant yell, and I was sure Alihak was dead.

The other soldier chased me. He was roughly the same height and build as me, tall and thin, and his hair was dark like mine, too. He came after me with a strange stiff shambling gait, almost like a zombie, and his arms were splattered with the blood of other people. I retreated down a long whitewashed hallway. It led to a window at the back of the hospital which was low to the ground. If I could make it to that window, I could escape; it opened onto a winding footpath that meandered into the tangled jungle.

Loosening his gait, the soldier quickened his pursuit. I turned a corner and ran down another long hallway, my bare feet slapping on the off-white tile floors, my footfalls echoing from the close walls. I ran past the open doors of unoccupied rooms, turned left, and then right. Footsteps somewhere behind me continued to pound the tile floor in pursuit. He was close, and he was going to overtake me before I reached the window. It was time to make a stand.

I ducked into an open door and waited for my pursuer. The room I had chosen for my stand was small, with antiseptic whitewashed walls. The only furnishings were a cot in the corner and a rounded mirror mounted on the wall, next to a shallow medicine cabinet. A little window, too small for a man to fit through, opened onto a bare inner courtyard. Through that window a blue-white sunbeam fell upon the smooth floor of my room. Outside, the abandoned, isolated courtyard contained a large birdbath or water fountain which occupied the otherwise empty central space. From the looks of the dead decorative bushes and dry stalks bordering the chipped walls, the courtyard had been forsaken for some time.

Inside the bowl of the fountain I could make out the tiny, matted gray corpse of a mock hummer, lying on its back in the muddy brown water. Perhaps the mock hummer thought krayfish lived in the bowl. The hummer needed them for food and reproduction. It would have fished for them until it starved. *Nothing survives in isolation*, I thought.

I opened the medicine cabinet and found a wicked looking scalpel with a six-inch, black diamond-edged blade. That would have to do if it came to a fight. I did my best to quiet my breathing. I waited.

An air of unreality pervaded the room, as if I were viewing it from a distance, or reading about it, rather than actually experiencing it. I glanced at the mirror. The startled reflection of a thin man with dark skin and wild brown hair glanced back.

The pursuer's footsteps slowed as the soldier approached the door. Should I retreat to the far wall and wait for my opponent to enter? Or should I jump into the hallway and confront him, in the hopes of catching him by surprise? The footsteps stopped just outside my door, so I backed up to the opposite wall and prepared to make my stand.

The enemy entered with deliberate caution, waving a razor sharp, black diamond-edged machete, and never taking his bloodshot eyes from me. We assumed identical stances, low crouches with weapons extended, ready to block or swing. I was breathing hard. So was he. I felt detached, and wondered, is this how an intelligent being behaves in its dying moment? My opponent looked gaunt and wasted.

His bloodshot eyes were surrounded by dark circles.
He was probably malnourished, and almost certainly
addicted to diamond root. We circled each other with
a shuffling gate, gauging one another. He was built
like me, so in physical terms, I figured we were evenly
matched, although he was probably far more
experienced in combat. I feinted with my scalpel in
my right hand. He stepped back to parry, then
stepped forward with a similar feint, showing
surprising dexterity. I backed to the wall and kept the
scalpel in front of me, and he withdrew by one step.
We shuffled again, feinted, withdrew, and circled. Our
weapons were so sharp that even one cut could end
the fight immediately. At last, I maneuvered so that
the mirror was at my back, on the side of my empty
left hand. The enemy feinted, and stepped back
again. With my free hand, I grabbed the mirror from
the wall and slung it at my opponent, charging at the
same time. The mirror struck a glancing blow to the
side of his head; stunned, the soldier twisted down
and away, momentarily off balance. His neck was
exposed. I slashed with my scalpel and decapitated
him with one stroke. A fountain of blood splashed

against the whitewashed wall, and the body slumped to the floor.

I felt like I had killed my double. I should have been in shock, but oddly enough, I had never thought so clearly in my entire life. I took the soldier's head and placed it back on his shoulders, then used his machete to skewer his head to his body in order to make sure it stayed in place; it looked much like the wound suffered by Korpusant. I placed the wicked-looking scalpel on the soldier's lap, to make sure my opponents knew this was the work of The Doctor. Finally, I placed the mirror directly in front of the corpse.

I departed the room, ran down a white tiled hall, and after making sure the coast was clear, climbed out a back window and lowered myself to the ground. Feeling alone and needing the company of my own kind, I followed a footpath into the surrounding bush and soon lost myself in the jungle, and so escaped Lutetia hospital.

THE LAST STAND

Standing in plain sight on Bimi Road was dangerous. I
was a wanted man with a bounty on my head. The
recent killing of the Joule Syndicate soldier at Lutetia
Hospital made me notorious, and now there were all
kinds of wild rumors. Some ascribed magical powers
to me. Others connected me to Korpusant back at
Bois Caiman: I was 'The Doctor,' and I resurrected
him, while another version confused resurrection with
becoming a zombie. Some claimed I was The Grand
Maestro, rather than Alihak. No disrespect intended
towards the late Professor, but that amused me,
because I actually would have liked to be known as
'The Only Miracle', given my fascination with
solipsism. Still other stories said Alihak was still alive
and impersonating me, or that he had died at Lutetia
Hospital of asthma, pneumonia, a pulmonary
embolism, or possibly La Fièvre Pourpre. It was just
wild stuff. In any case, the killing at Lutetia Hospital
had made me infamous. There were primitive black
and white posters of me plastered by the Joule

Syndicate on the walls and fences of Ambreville and the Bimi waterfront: 'Wanted, dead or alive.' What a strange phrase! Who would want me when I was dead? It seemed incredible that I should have a reputation for being bloodthirsty, and it seemed even more incredible that the event at Lutetia Hospital should draw any attention at all, given the background of constant chaos, anarchy, and brutal violence going on in the Nouveau Haitian bush. Mercenaries had slaughtered a bunch of hapless students at the hospital, and instead of an outcry directed against them, there were wanted posters for me? I was one of the least bloodthirsty people in the world! Nevertheless, there was a motive for the posters. It was a JS mercenary I killed at Lutetia Hospital, and now Joule wanted his revenge. He was almost certainly the one responsible for the posters. His troops might have been poor, but Joule was very rich, and he was not about to put up with what I had done to one of his soldiers.

And now? The JS mercenary was dead. Armstrong was dead. Alihak was dead. The University had been burned to the ground. Everyone else was blown to the eight winds, including Victoria and Professor Koppes. I was left standing in plain sight on the Bimi Road, bare feet planted on the cool, closely fitted octagonal stones. I understood the danger, but I could not help myself. *'Nothing survives in isolation,'* I thought. I was alone and it was time. It was time in every sense of the word.

My traveling days were over. I had been The Doctor and I had been a Valedictorian. My intentions had almost always been good, even though I once did something terrible enough to earn the bounty on my head; but after all was said and done, well, it was time. It was time for the last farewell, here on the banks of the great Bimi River, next to the creaking wooden pier.

In temporal terms, it was the day of the week called Market Day, and the Market Day vendors had set up along the riverside at dawn, and now the rows of brightly colored booths displayed fresh produce: limes, carrots, potatoes, and red beans. The poorer ones could not afford booths, so they spread their meager wares upon threadbare blankets. Although it was still early, the humidity was incredible this close to the river. I was thirsty, but I did not have the money to pay for a drink, and it was a bad idea to go into the river.

Even though the humidity and heat were oppressive, Nouveau Haitians made a point of staying away from the water, and it was easy to understand why. Several dead creatures had been found floating close to the pier recently; since there were no visible signs of injury or disease, that suggested the creatures had been victims of electrocution, which meant a dangerous white whip might be in the area. Although they knew about the danger, instinct still drew Nouveau Haitians to gather by the banks. I laughed to myself. The old saying was true: *'The soul migrates to water.'* Despite the danger of standing in plain sight, here I stood, drawn to the Bimi as well, at the end of my own personal migration.

The low blue-white sun cast long shadows across the Bimi Road, and I could already feel the intense rays on my dark skin. My shadow would shorten as the sun climbed, until it stood directly beneath me. Maybe the same process would hold true for my life. Here I would make my stand, here on the outskirts of a boisterous Market Day crowd, by the banks of the Bimi River; here, with bare feet planted on the smooth gray octagonal stones of the Road. I was a peripatetic with a penchant for violence, but I was too tired to continue the fight. My traveling days were over. It was time for a resolution. It was time.

Nearby, a gray-haired lunatic sat on the hard packed dirt, unshaven, dressed in filthy rags. If I persisted and endured for a few more years, that would be me.

A vendor hawked slabs of lectra ray to the Market Day crowd, and I trembled with hunger. The odor of the cooked, firm white flesh topped with minced ginger permeated the humid air, and made me salivate. Apparently my rumbling stomach did not believe in solipsism. Despite my overpowering hunger, I stood still, and tightened the cord holding up my tattered pants. I was still thin, my face long, my hair dark. Most people considered me a good looking man. Unfortunately, my clothes and bare feet told another story: I was a handsome impoverished middle-aged man, and poor men with no prospects were as common as arachnoflies in Ambreville. I owned nothing but my time and the space upon which I stood. My biggest concern was that someone would recognize me.

Some high clouds moved in, but even with a hazy overcast the small blue-white sunlight felt intense. The sun was near its zenith and my shadow shortened so that it now stood almost directly beneath me. I held my place as the Market Day crowd swelled.

Preoccupied men and shopping women bumped and jostled me without apology as they hurried past to do their errands. They took me for one of the mentally ill, or a beggar, or perhaps both.

A woman in a red checked dress stopped to offer me a crust of bread. Upon her narrow wrist she wore a bracelet of violet beads, with a spot of brown and yellow upon each one; small globes encircling her wrist in an endless round. She was quite attractive, with short, straight dark hair and a small nose. I accepted her offering of charity with a grateful nod. *I eat, therefore I am*, I joked to myself, and I ate the bread with pleasure.

A middle-aged businessman with greasy, slicked back hair walked past us. He eyed the pretty woman and paid no attention to me. I was secretly pleased the woman ignored the businessman. He wore a dark blue shirt with a soiled white collar, red tie, mustard yellow suspenders, and stained slacks. A machete was sheathed on his hip. I remembered him. He was a member of the Joule Syndicate. He was the one who chased Alihak up the stairs. I balled my fists and clenched my teeth, but avoided eye contact with the killer. The businessman walked past us, paused, and turned to face me.

"Do I know you?" He squinted at me.

I stared at my feet.

"Who are you?" He glanced at a vendor's stall some distance away. A crudely drawn wanted poster for me was displayed on its awning.

I shifted my weight from one foot to another.

129

"Hey, buddy!" He smirked and stepped towards me, placing one hand on the hilt of his knife. "Ever been to Lutetia Hospital?"

I broke towards the densest part of the crowd in the direction of the river. I ran for my life, bare feet slapping the stones.

He ran after me, shouting my name. Several other men and boys in the crowd took up the pursuit.

So much for solipsism, I thought. The external world was coming for me whether I believed in it or not.

"It's The Doctor! Stop that man!"

With a swimming motion I made my way through the crowd, pushing past one body after another. A group of young men- presumably on the Ambreville police payroll, since they were too well-dressed for typical Nouveau Haitians- joined the chase. I cleared the crowd but there was no way I was going to lose my pursuers. Ahead, the gunmetal gray waters of the broad Bimi stretched before me. No one would risk the danger of following me into the Bimi, not even for a bounty. I reached the bank ahead of them, and dove headfirst into the river.

When I surfaced a short distance away, a crowd had already gathered on the bank. I swam a short distance downstream, and most of them followed on land. I let the current carry me, and elation rose in my heart, a sense of ecstasy, of standing outside of myself-

My world disappeared in a blue flash.

The electrical shock hit me like a hammer blow, simultaneously striking every part of my body. The world gradually returned, like a developing photograph. I felt as if I had fallen into hardening amber. I saw myself as if from a distance, and realized I had been paralyzed by electricity, the animating force of life. Disembodied voices spoke. Water closed over my head, and I felt a falling away-

THE COFFIN

My awareness floated outside my body as I watched young men use poles, gaffs, and ropes to retrieve me from the Bimi. After pulling my body onto dry land, the well-dressed, well-groomed youths immediately set to arguing over the bounty. They dragged my corpse to the center of the market, and the businessman joined the argument, claiming he saw me first, so he deserved the reward. They pushed and pulled, and onlookers gathered, hoping to catch a glimpse of the notorious man known as 'The Doctor.'

Nearby, the attractive woman in the red checked dress paid no attention to the arguing males. She slowly shook her head. "Such a pity," she said to a petite, dark haired woman standing next to her. The dark haired woman agreed. Next to her, the filthy gray-haired lunatic pressed his gnarled hands together over his heart, and addressing my prone body, said "I am so sorry for you."

A boy clutching a blue-white toy ball pushed his way to the front. "Let me see him!"

"Me first!" his twin exclaimed, shoving and jockeying for position.

"Hold on!" one of the young men said. "Now everyone, wait a minute!" He conferred with the businessman next to him. They came to an agreement, and then sent the twins on an errand. Men and women, young and old alike, milled around my body in the hope catching a glimpse, but the crush of the crowd made it difficult to get a good look.

The twins returned almost dancing with joy, and they cavorted around an old Miner veteran who dragged a narrow wooden coffin behind him. The young men placed my body in the coffin, and although it was a tight fit, the coffin worked well enough for their purpose. They stood it on end in a standing position, and now everyone could enjoy a better view.

"Is that the Grand Maestro?" one youth asked.

The businessman laughed. "I doubt it."

"That's The Doctor!" another youth added.

Look," the Miner said, "he's still alive. His right bicep twitched."

The businessman hooked his thumbs in his yellow suspenders, and shrugged. "Discharging synapses."

PEACE

Peace filled my heart. I accepted my relations with others and my dependency upon them without resentment. I felt no anger towards the white whip either. It expressed its own unique nature within its environment as a matter of instinct, just as I did in my own environments; the difference was that I could rise above my instincts through acts of kindness and compassion. 'I think, therefore I am' did not justify solipsism, since an underlying truth was equally valid: 'I am, therefore we are.' I was embarrassed to have so few acts of kindness to my credit, but impressed by how many were done by others: Victoria was famous for her charitable giving and concern for the poor; Armstrong was tremendously generous to me when I first arrived at the University; and finally, the woman in the red checked dress received my profound gratitude.

I knew the answer to the question. I knew how I would behave in my dying moment. It was time to make my last stand. In my mind, I rose and straightened. Charged with a sense of well-being and belonging, I ascended into an electrical center of shimmering blue-white light...

THE RETURN

... And descended back into my body in a soundless purple implosion. My head, my nose, my lungs, my heart- all throbbed and hummed with manic, irritable energy. I opened my eyes. A petite, dark haired woman with dark brown eyes stood face to face with me, holding a small pipette in her hand and smiling.

"Miss me?"

It was Victoria! With nothing more than the force of her personality and her reputation for being a witch, she had cleared the superstitious crowd far away enough from my coffin to perform the same trick I used on Korpusant so long ago. The energy I experienced was from the diamond root crystals blown into my nose, throat, and lungs; and now, the white whip's electricity was inside me too. Its parasites and the water of the Bimi were inside me. They animated me to affirm life, both today and in my own future personal migration, many years hence.

Now, it was my turn to return. Dead or alive, I was back.

After coughing hard and regaining control of my breathing, I stepped from the coffin and faced the crowd. I will never forget the expressions of slack jawed amazement on their faces. Everyone was positively dumbfounded. It looked to me like the mother-of-all teachable moments.

"Victoria?"

"Yes?"

"I have an idea."

The Spider

The spider paused to investigate a crack in the brown hardpan. Inserting long, spindly front legs into the recess, the spider found neither prey nor means of reproduction, so it skittered a short distance across the hot flat surface to look into the next crack. Hunger kept it seeking. It did not know or care about drought, dry winds, the lake which once covered this dry ground, or the waterhole in the distance; the spider continued its hunt across the octagonal pattern of cracks with a sense of urgency, yet no sense of time. It knew only the blazing bright light, shadow, and the sharp creosote odors of the land.

There! The olfactory receptors on its front legs detected the barest hint of an exciting scent. Something lurked in the next crack, something irresistible. Instinct served as memory, and it demanded a stealthy approach and total concentration.

In its excitement, the spider disregarded the increasingly strong vibrations of the ground, rumblings the equivalent of an earthquake in its small world. Something enormous approached, but the urge to flee was trumped by the overwhelming temptation.

Within the crack, a small metallic blue, eight-legged beetle detected the approaching spider's odor. With slow, methodical steps, it labored towards the rim of the crack, and the light. Wonderful, wonderful, the spider was so close-

A shadow eclipsed the bright blue-lilac light for both spider and beetle-

And like a thunderclap from on high, an enormous brown boot came down upon the spider.

WATERMAN

A twist of the boot smashed the spider into the hardpan of Phosphor Plain. After he finished grinding the tiny creature into the dirt, Lord Waterman and I stood side by side. Inwardly, I winced when the spider died. It was cruel. It was thoughtless and unnecessary. Unlike me, Waterman had never bothered to ponder how a small being behaved in its dying moment.

"Crush the enemy," he said.

"How?" I asked. Next to the heel of Waterman's dusty brown jack boot, a blue glint on the ground caught my eye. It was a tiny beetle, retreating into a crack.

"With overwhelming force."

We resumed walking side by side upon the dry Phosphor Plain. I am tall and thin, but Waterman towered over me. He was huge, with dark skin, broad shoulders and a barrel chest, and he was quite a bit younger than me. He was self-centered and focused, the physical incarnation of applied force. He came from the second largest city on Nouveau Haitiah, and like most of those inhabitants, he dressed more formally than the climate warranted, wearing a black waistcoat made of thin material, a tan shirt, and brown pants. "Crush the Children's Fund," he continued. "Crush the Fraternité Internationale des Ouvriers en Electricité. Crush the Miners. We have the numbers. No need to be subtle."

I wiped a drop of sweat from the end of my nose. The man by my side was thoughtless and cruel, but definitely not subtle. He was setting me up for a betrayal. He would not only seek to slaughter the enemy like that spider, he would eventually do the same to my followers, the Feux Follets, and then he would come for me. He was an easy read, an open book, but that did not make my situation any less perilous.

"When you killed that spider," I said, "you also killed a nearby beetle."

He furrowed his brows. "What do you mean?"

"Everything on Nouveau Haitiah is connected, you know. The beetle needed to be consumed by the spider in order to insert its viral phages. It needed the spider in order to reproduce."

"Yes, well, you make connections, I break them."

"Interdependence-"

"- Did you know," he interrupted, "that the Phosphor Plain used to be a jungle? My troops burned it. Now it makes a good place for me to put my foot down and crush my enemies. This is the perfect place for a battle- flat and open for miles, with no cover- so it will be purely a matter of strength and numbers." He patted my shoulder. "Book learning is impressive, Oba. That is why you are my Surgeon General. I cannot read, but I know how to use my boot. And that is why I am Lord."

I gazed at distant thunderheads beyond the Phosphor Plain. *Waterman does not appreciate interdependency*, I thought. *He sees everything in terms of opposing forces. That weakness might be exploited.*

Working for Waterman was the price for achieving my goal- to finally stop the fighting once and for all, and bring peace to Nouveau Haitiah. Waterman stood in my way. After this battle, I would have to deal with the lawyer Burnette, who controlled the Ambreville Police and the legal system, as well as the businessman Joule, but the military piece could be resolved right here. Waterman, in turn, intended to use me to win this last battle and achieve his own goal, sole ruler of Nouveau Haitiah. My fanatical soldiers in black pajamas- the Feux Follets Cult- would provide the decisive cutting edge to his Lord's Army of Resistance.

The LAR kept reappearing in my life. The first time was after I crawled out of the pool so long ago and met Remy, and he led me to the LAR camp near Bois Caiman. At that time, I performed what seemed like a resurrection on a man, Korpusant. A few years later, when Victoria brought me back to life after I jumped into the Bimi and was shocked by a white whip, and I said, "I have an idea," it was this: I used the strange, mixed up rumors about how I was The Doctor who performed a resurrection to encourage the belief that I had supernatural powers. Of course, my very public return from the dead a few years ago at the Bimi pier helped the rumors along, thanks to Victoria. Naturally I placed myself at the head of this new religion, and the believers became fanatical followers who were initially called the Will-o'-the-Wisps; later they would be better known as the Feux Follets. I used the cult to rise to second-in-command in the LAR alliance in order to achieve my own goals. Now my power made me a threat to the commander, Lord Waterman.

The small, intense sun threw off a bright, blue-white light today. It brought out the violet undertones on the undersides of the distant thunderheads; hard on the eyes, but very pretty. It almost glowed, as if the ultraviolet spectrum was about to break into the visible one.

Maybe it would rain. I licked my lips. The Plain was so dry. I was thirsty all the time, and so were the troops. Our army was the largest put together in a long time, and we had won a chain of impressive victories; however, logistics were a nightmare with an army this big, and right now, we had no water supply. Perhaps the soul migrated to water, but the body wanted to migrate to it just as much. The last remaining effective fighting force- an alliance of The Children's Fund, the FIOE, and the Miners- were encamped next to a natural spring, the only source of potable water in the area. They could hide behind their makeshift fortifications almost indefinitely.

"We have superior numbers," Waterman said. "We can't wait any longer. We have to attack. What do you suggest, Surgeon General?"

I smiled. He used that title to appeal to my vanity. But he was right about the need to make a decision. The soldiers were volatile under normal circumstances; without water, they could mutiny or desert. What should I recommend? I licked my lips again, and touched the canteen on my hip. Empty.

"An assault on that position would be murderous. They will not attack us. I suggest we leave a blocking force and send most of the army against their home territory, Combray."

"Really?" Waterman stopped walking and shielded his eyes as he gazed at the enemy fieldworks. "If we withdraw, our opponents will see us. Some of our troops will desert and our army could melt away into the jungle."

I nodded and pretended to agree. What he really meant was that *his* army would melt away- not my followers. Waterman controlled a lot of troops, but as the figurehead of the cult, my Feux Follets believed I could cure death itself, so they would remain loyal to me regardless of circumstances.

Waterman rubbed his chin. "The enemy could overwhelm any blocking force that stays behind, assuming our men hold their position in the first place. No. The whole campaign could come apart if we do not finish them." He shook a clenched fist. "It ends here."

"It ends here," I echoed. I wondered if that blue beetle felt disappointment.

"Surgeon General, what if we attacked at night?"

I hesitated. "It would be a bloodbath."

"Bloody, yes, but we would win."

"We would take enormous casualties." A salty bead of sweat ran down my nose. I was so thirsty.

"It would be a great victory. We would use overwhelming force and crush them. Your Feux Follets wear black anyway. They would be perfect for leading the night assault."

I nodded and swallowed hard. Waterman was an uneducated, physically intimidating man, but he was no fool.

"The Feux Follets will follow you anywhere. You will lead the assault."

It was a clever plan. Attrition would thin out the Feux Follets ranks, and there was a good chance I would be killed in the bargain. If I survived, my power base would be so diminished, it would be easy for Waterman to finish me off and take sole control of Nouveau Haitiah. I needed to stall for time. "Let's negotiate first."

Waterman dismissed the idea with a wave of a hand. "I prefer the direct approach."

"It could work," I persisted.

He took a deep breath. "What are you talking about? They don't trust us, and we don't trust them."

"Yes," I said, warming to my idea, "but we could make them think we are considering withdrawing, you know, let them see how desperate we are for water. It would help convince them to lower their guard. Our night assault would be a complete surprise."

"I like it," Waterman said. He clasped his big hands behind his back and puffed out his chest.

"They should never have rolled the dice with you, Lord Waterman." I regretted this as soon as I said it. I have never been good at insincere flattery.

"Right! Let's do this, Surgeon General. Just one thing."

"What is that?"

He gave me a big smile and a slap on the back. "You will lead the negotiations."

I looked down and smoothed the front of my shirt. This was not just unanticipated. This was disastrous. We both knew coming into close contact with the other side was risky. Negotiating was almost as dangerous as leading an attack, maybe worse. "You are our leader-"

"- And I will wait here," he finished. "I will send an orderly out there with you to carry our flag. Oh, and while we're at it, let's send The Official Hostess, Victoria, with you."

He turned and returned to the troops. As I stared at his back, I made a vow to myself: *one day, Waterman, I will mount your skull on a hat rack.* My own viciousness caught me off guard; to think I used to be a quiet guy who liked to read books! Becoming powerful in order to save myself and others had changed me, and now, not only was I unable to save anyone, but I was in danger of losing my life. A sudden gust of wind blew gritty dust in my face. Although the thunderstorms were still far off, the winds from the downdrafts were reaching us even here.

"I hope you brought an umbrella," Waterman said. "Looks like rain."

BALL LIGHTNING

Victoria and I were in camp, preparing to walk into the middle of the Phosphor Plain and meet with the other side. Since coming together in the LAR we had become careful allies. I wanted our relationship to be more than an alliance, but she always kept me at an arm's distance; of course, that was true of the way she treated men in general, so even though I knew I was being unrealistic, that distance kept my hopes alive. Remy was supposed to come with us onto the Plain, but he was arguing with Quartermaster Faraday, a stocky, bowlegged man with curly blond hair and rosy cheeks, about some missing provisions. They were both so short they were able to argue eye to eye. Faraday put his finger into Remy's chest and accused him of pilfering, but before they could resolve it, a low collective moan of despair swept through our troops. There was a general movement towards the perimeter facing the opposing army and the empty plain.

"What is it?" Remy asked me. "Is it a surprise attack?" Faraday shrugged and shook his head.

"I don't know Remy," I replied. "I don't think so. Come on!" I slapped his back, and pulled the corpulent orderly away from the Quartermaster. We crowded forward with the rest of the soldiers to see what was happening. The Lord's Army of Resistance had been incorporated into Lord Waterman's force, so most of the LAR and Feux Follets wore black, but at least Remy and the Quartermaster had sense enough not to dress like the rest. Remy still wore a faded, dirty green graduation gown.

The assembled troops all watched the middle of the Phosphor Plain. I saw Fernal, Current, Voltson, Quartermaster Faraday, and others I recognized from the Feux Follets. Some pointed. Some knelt. Victoria joined us, and since both she and Remy were short, we pushed our way to the front for a better view. Remy rolled his eyes in terror and pulled up his gown to cover his eyes. I soon saw the cause of his dismay.

Halfway between the two armies, in the middle of the no-man's land, a bluish-white ball of lightning rolled across the hardpan. It followed a random, erratic course, wandering this way and that, until it abruptly discharged with a boom and an actinic flash.

A commotion, followed by yells and a shout, drew my attention to a nearby knot of men who were struggling with one of their own. The man broke free and ran into no-man's land, towards the place where the ball lightning had discharged. He swung his arms in an odd motion, as if he were swimming through the air. I recognized him. It was Mister Liberty. There was no mistaking him. It was the same man I met back at the LAR camp near Bois Caiman. He wore the black pajamas of the Feux Follets, and still fashioned his hair into spikes, and now he even carried a lit torch.

Lord Waterman ordered the troops to hold their positions. Some had been smoking diamond root, so they were in a highly suggestible state. Who knew what they would make of the ball lightning or Mister Liberty running around in the middle of Phosphor Plain? He finally stopped running and pointed in our direction with his free hand. Later, Faraday told me Mister Liberty was dedicating himself to me, but I

never heard it, and I saw the whole thing. Mister
Liberty pulled a ceramic canteen from his belt with his
free hand, and then doused himself with a liquid while
holding the torch high over his head. He repeated the
process with another canteen until he was thoroughly
soaked. And then Mister Liberty touched his robe
with fire. He went up in flames quickly, burning
brightly, and crackling like a human torch.

THE TALKS

A short time later, Victoria, Remy, one of my most devoted followers, Fernal, and I walked into no-man's land. We stood midway between the two armies, but a good distance from the still smoldering body of Mister Liberty, and waited for our opponent's negotiators. A thin plume of greasy black smoke rose from the corpse into the bright blue-white sky. The light was intense this afternoon, and it made me squint. Remy carried our flag, which had a blue field and a stylized mock hummer.

"That was horrible," Victoria said, covering her mouth with her hand and shaking her head. Remy agreed.

"*Incroyable*," Fernal said in his deep voice.

"I have never seen anything like it," I added.

She gave Fernal a sidelong glance while addressing me. "The Feux Follets are fanatics. They want to martyr themselves for you."

"Why? What is the point of martyrdom?" I asked. I slowly shook my head and took a deep breath. "I want to stop the fighting. I want to bring peace to Nouveau Haitiah. That kind of sacrifice makes no sense."

"Neither of you get it," Fernal said irritably.

Remy refused to look at Fernal. He wanted nothing to do with the Feux Follets. "Do you think the Children's Fund saw it?" Remy asked me.

I grimaced. "How could they miss it?"

"Of course they saw it," Victoria said at the same time. "Maybe we can use it to our advantage?"

"What will they think?" Remy would not let it go.

"Well, let's ask them," I replied. "Here they come."

Five figures crossed the opposing perimeter and walked towards us with a bounce in their step. Obviously they were optimistic. The ongoing anarchy of Nouveau Haitiah had lasted longer than anyone could remember, and this parley might prevent a battle. Surely their small delegation assumed the same as us; an assault was unlikely, yet surrender was out of the question. In another minute we would meet each other in the middle of no-man's land.

The petite woman in the middle, Odette, wore a saffron sarong. She was barefoot and little taller than a child. Odette carried a blue macoute- a handbag- with a pattern of stylized fountains on it. Her pale complexion was unusual for a Nouveau Haitian, given the intensity of the small blue white-sun, and her softly curled ginger hair also distinguished her from the rest of the population. One of the negotiators, a middle-aged man with broad shoulders, wore his long brown hair in a pony tail. He carried the flag for the Children's Fund faction, a saffron banner with a fountain of water at its center. He was flanked by a businessman from the Joule Syndicate. On the other side, an old Miner carried a flag with two concentric circles, along with a man from the FIOE, a Colonel Swain, supposedly representing the workers of the world. I liked seeing different flags. It suggested their army had split loyalties.

"I know her," Victoria said in a voice low enough not to be heard by the other delegation. "That is Odette. She is the daughter of Commissar Ampere, and she is a malfacteur."

"A what?"

"A malfacteur- a specialist in malevolent magic. She is the witch for the Children's Fund."

"I recognize the name," I said. Although I did not believe anyone was a witch, I knew Fernal and Remy did, and Victoria cultivated that belief about herself, so I let the matter slide. "Odette supposedly killed Korpusant with a knife through the top of his skull. That seems highly unlikely to me. By the way, Victoria, she now calls herself 'The Unofficial Hostess.'"

Victoria narrowed her eyes. She encouraged others to address her as 'The Official Hostess.' Odette was clearly mocking of her. "She interprets omens for the Fund," Victoria said. "The witchcraft may be a scam, but she is strong in other ways. She is smart. She is clever. She is probably crazy. Her specialties are powders and poisons."

"Great."

"We should be safe out in the open," Victoria said matter-of-factly, as if dealing with poisons was routine.

I wondered about Victoria's so-called specialties, but put my concerns aside for the time being. Remy stammered something about spells. Fernal looked concerned and shifted his weight from one foot to the other. Victoria laughed lightheartedly. "Don't worry. You have me to protect you."

An unexpected gust from a distant storm caused the flag to snap and flutter wildly for a moment, catching Remy off guard, but he maintained his grip and turned to me. "What about the Miners? What about the FIOE?"

I shrugged. "You never know with the Miners. They smoke more diamond root than anyone I have ever seen. They are unpredictable. And the FIOE are few in number and too disorganized."

Remy planted the flag in a crack in the hardpan, indicating our desire to parley. A tiny glint of metallic blue caught my eye as a beetle disappeared deeper into a crack.

They planted their flags and the malfacteur spoke to me first: *"Je m'appelle Odette.* I represent Commissar Ampere, the leader of our coalition." She winked at me as if we were sharing a secret. "It's about time you and I had a talk, don't you think?" I agreed. "This is Colonel Swain, our second-in-command" she continued, indicating the FIOE delegate. He acknowledged us with a curt nod. The Colonel wore camouflage overalls and maintained an erect military bearing. He had a crew cut and a dark pencil thin mustache, and sported an ostentatious ring, a gaudy blue gemstone that flashed with reflected sunlight. His small faction had a reputation for siding with whoever was winning at the time.

The Miner jabbered nonsense. He was clearly out of his head. It must have been diamond root. Odette rolled her eyes and gave me a 'see what I have to deal with' look.

The businessman for the Joule Syndicate introduced himself as well. The young man from the Syndicate wore a stained white shirt, mustard yellow suspenders, and dirty black slacks. He stared openly at Victoria. She gave him her most winning smile, and I am pretty sure he was smitten then and there. She had that effect on men. Stranger yet, Remy stared at Victoria a moment longer than appropriate. I had never seen him do that before, or even express an interest in women. I used to believe he feared Victoria. Now I realized Remy adored her.

"Who are you?" Odette asked. Odette knew of me and Victoria, of course, but asking that question about identity always gave the questioner power. It put the person asking in charge, making that person the arbiter and judge of identity. Victoria and Odette were two of the most powerful women on Nouveau Haitiah, and now they were close for the first time. It occurred to me they might be jealous of one another.

Remy stammered and introduced us, adding that we represented Lord Waterman. He introduced Victoria as The Official Hostess and me as Surgeon General, but did not refer to me as 'The Doctor.' I was sure they knew anyway.

"What is the purpose of this parley?" Odette asked.

"We are here to discuss your surrender," I replied.

Odette laughed. "Don't be ridiculous. Let's talk truce. You may leave Phosphor Plain without fear of attack."

"You know we will not agree to that," I said.

"Well, our surrendering is out of the question," Odette said with a toss of the head. "It is a foolish notion."

"We have the superior position," the Joule delegate added.

"Your army is starving," I said. "We have food. Lord Waterman will authorize us to share."

"Your army is dying of thirst," Odette countered, "and we have a spring. You look like you could use a drink, Surgeon General." With one graceful arm she extended a flask in my direction. Wary of her reputation with poisons, I politely declined.

At that moment, the rumble of a distant thunderstorm reached us. "Hear that?" I asked, cupping my ear with one hand. "See those clouds?" I took a deep breath. "Smells like rain."

Instead of replying, she kicked up a little cloud of dust from the hardpan and hummed to herself. The Miner jabbered some more. His eyes were dilated. We all ignored him.

Odette smiled and looked down at her feet. She idly traced a pattern on the hardpan with her toe. "Did you see the fireball? It predicts the death of important men." The Miner's eyelids fluttered at the mention of the fireball. Remy made a quick sign of the crossroads.

"No one cares about omens," I said. "We have more soldiers, and that is all that matters."
"More thirsts to quench," the pony-tailed man from the Children's Fund rejoined. He turned towards the Miner and his eyes widened in alarm.

The Miner's eyes rolled up into his head and he started shaking hard. He trembled and collapsed to the ground, twisting and writhing and frothing at the mouth.

"The fool took too much diamond root," Victoria said. Odette shook her head in exasperation. Fernal stared straight ahead as if it were not happening. Remy wrung his hands. We had all seen this kind of thing before. I knew about it from personal experience, back at Bois Caiman. "We need to take him back to our camp," Odette said.

"What about the negotiation?" I asked.

The Miner's convulsions became more violent.

"Well, we can't just leave him there." Odette attempted to give him a drink from her canteen, but the Miner was shaking too hard.

"I will carry him back to the lines. Will you help me, Odette?" the man with the pony tail asked. Since he came from the Children's Fund, he was Odette's primary supporter. I began to suspect none of them trusted each other. This was good for me.

Odette agreed. "Victoria," she said, "you know a lot about diamond root. Maybe you can help too. Will you come with us?"

Victoria flipped a strand of her black hair from her shoulder. The comment about diamond root was a dig implying Victoria was an addict, but it was in fact true that she knew a lot about it. Going to the opponent's camp was dangerous for Victoria, but the fact that she was The Official Hostess commanded respect from the male soldiers, not to mention her reputation for being a witch. "Of course. Remy, help us carry the old man."

"We will be right back," Odette said. They departed with the Miner.

"Lord Waterman wants a battle," I said to the businessman and the FIOE representative, Colonel Swain. "It would be a great slaughter."

"So does Commissar Ampere," the businessman agreed. "They both want to be the new Big Man. There is no profit in that for the rest of us."

"They would have us kill each other for no good reason," Swain observed.

I folded my arms. "Surely we can do something about this."

"The problem is Waterman and Ampere," Fernal asserted in his deep voice.

"The problem is Waterman and Ampere," Colonel Swain echoed. I nodded in agreement.

"Odette represents Ampere. She is his daughter," the businessman added cagily. "Maybe we can come up with a solution before Victoria and Odette return. It should be easier to negotiate without them."

I clapped my hands. "I have an idea."

RESOLUTION

The negotiation was a smashing success, and in a sense, the omen of the ball lightning came true. Waterman gave a brief struggle, and made some loud and vehement protests, but that was the last time I heard him speak. The exchange of Waterman for Ampere went without a hitch, although I heard Odette posed a problem in the other camp. They let her escape, which was a mistake, but an understandable one; when cornered, she made a compelling case for her freedom by brandishing a machete in one hand and a vial of poisonous mist in the other.

After the exchange of Waterman for Ampere, the two armies joined in the middle of the plain for a splendid party. We brought the food. They brought the water. The Miners brought the diamond root. Victoria objected to what followed- she detested betrayal and what she knew was about to happen to Waterman and Ampere- but of course the men ignored her. Her protests generated some ill will, and with a little gentle urging on my part, Victoria later fled into a self-imposed exile at Colombe Habitation, near the mouth of the Bimi. I objected to what happened to Waterman and Ampere on principle, but honestly, I did not protest very hard. After drumming and singing and other festivities we concluded with a barbecue. Naturally, Waterman and Ampere were the guests of honor, although being hog-tied and gagged prevented them from participating. Maybe I should not have done this, but I kept both skulls and later mounted them on a hat rack in my office.

I went on to enjoy many fine moments in my path to becoming sole ruler of Nouveau Haitiah, but recalling this coup gave me my greatest pleasure. I saved many lives that day at the cost of only two or three, depending on whether the count included one small spider.

It never did rain.

VICTORIA

THE OFFICIAL HOSTESS

A swarm of metallic red arachnoflies buzzed outside the great bay window, banging against the panes with the dumb, unwitting persistence of mindless parasites. From my perspective at the head of the table, and as the Official Hostess, they crowned the head of one dinner guest with a halo, as if The Doctor or The Grand Maestro or The Only Miracle or whatever he called himself these days was really His Holiness, patron saint of pests. But why did the arachnoflies want in? Perhaps the lights drew them from the damp Nouveau Haitian night; or perhaps they were attracted by the gingered aroma of the appetizer waiting to be served, although the food was still covered in its ceramic serving dish- the finest tableware in all of Nouveau Haitiah, by the way; but I preferred to imagine the arachnoflies were drawn to him, sensing The Doctor would make an exceptionally fine Host. Good luck with that!

As the Hostess of tonight's dinner and this fine and final political summit, I dressed in my own version of finery. I wore my light, classically cut dove grey dress because it complemented my dark skin and dark hair to perfection. The subdued coral hue of my belt set off the gray of my dress and the rich tones of my smooth skin, while simultaneously accentuating my slim figure. My soft leather shoes completed the ensemble. The shoes were actually the best part of the outfit, although I doubted anyone else appreciated them. In any case, I did not depend solely on my attractiveness or sense of style to make an event such as this a success, but of course, image counts, and a certain amount of vanity was to be expected from The Official Hostess of Nouveau Haitiah.

The Doctor wore pressed khaki trousers and a cream colored shirt. The others were similarly attired. At least the lawyer, Burnette, dressed well. The fat business tycoon, Joule, wore a rumpled black suit, and obviously did not care about his appearance or physique, with the exception of his generous and well groomed salt and pepper mustache. General Swain had a crew cut and dark, pencil thin mustache. He wore an olive shirt and dark green slacks, and an ostentatious ring on his finger, a gaudy blue gemstone. I sniffed in disapproval. It clashed with his crisp outfit. Odette wore a simple brown dress and carried her macoute, a light blue handbag with a stylized pattern of fountains on it. Every person at this table was dangerous in their own way; none more dangerous than the female malfacteur.

Ignoring the obnoxious thump of the arachnoflies, I entertained my guests by making gracious talk. The Doctor remained silent. That was good. He knew his position in the scheme of things. On the one hand, I might need him later as a potential ally; on the other hand, almost anyone else at the table might make a better one. In the meantime, I intended to make sure he knew how I felt about him. He was responsible for my exile. He claimed it was self-imposed, but the truth is, he forced me into it after that infamous negotiation between those armies on Phosphor Plain.

And after all I had done for him! Why, I saved his life at Bois Caiman, the first time we met, and again at Ambreville! And he repaid me by banishing me, just because I took a principled, moral stand after that infamous negotiation.

He banished me to this isolated place, Colombe Habitation, here near the ocean and the mouth of the Bimi, so very far from the political center at Ambreville. Despite its remoteness, the traditional neutrality of the site and its isolation eventually became a source of strength. It looked even more attractive as a site for the summit after the latest severe outbreak of the hemorrhagic fever, La Fièvre Pourpre, in Combray. Now the ultimate political resolution remained to be worked out. At last, the tables were turned in my favor. We were all here at Colombe Habitation, on my turf. The fighting ended after the negotiation, but now the resolution was to be reached among the last players standing, and I was in the enviable position of being the Official Hostess of Nouveau Haitiah.

"Care to try the appetizer? It's a surprise." Focusing upon the ornate platter, I held my perfect smile a moment longer than necessary, allowing the guests to appreciate my refined features: my petite nose, even white teeth, and widely set dark brown eyes, accentuated with just a touch of eyeliner. After taking official possession of Colombe Habitation a few years ago, I had let my hair grow, and now it was shoulder-length, wavy, and hung upon my shoulder just so. With one hand, I gestured for my corpulent attendant, Remy, to unveil the covered dish. With the other, I absentmindedly fingered my necklace of Nouveau Haitian pearls, drawing the gazes of the others to the smooth skin of my throat. I dipped my fingers into a small dark blue bowl of sea water and touched the pearls, enhancing their nacreous luster. Such beautiful pearls! Not only were they uncommon, they were my only accessory, and contrasted wonderfully with my outfit; besides, fondling the pearls reminded the guests of my reputation; many Nouveau Haitians believed my pearls were magical. Many also believed I was a witch.

Unlike Odette, I was not. On occasion I would conduct a séance, but that hardly made me a witch. I only cultivated that reputation because I needed it. I did not deceive or mislead anyone. I just let them believe what they wanted to believe. I had to, because I commanded no army. I possessed little wealth. My powers derived from my charisma, my glamorous image, my association with charities and worthy social causes, my personal popularity- and, of course, fear of my reputed supernatural powers.

The men reminded me of parasitic pests gathered around the table; nevertheless, they treated me with respect. So did Odette. My servant, however, ignored my charms. We argued about this earlier. Remy considered himself a member of the staff of Colombe Habitation, and therefore attached to the institution rather than any particular person; however, my status as Official Hostess meant the Colombe Habitation staff worked for me, so therefore, Remy was my servant. I even paid him! Of course, the money came from someone else, but that was beside the point.

Despite his surly disposition, lack of training, and occasional rebelliousness, I believe Remy cared for me, the staff, and Colombe Habitation traditions. Remy had never been a fighter, but who would have guessed he would end up as a house domestic? He seemed to have found his place in the world. Like the other members of the staff- the cook, maid, groundskeeper, guards, and half a dozen others- he wore a navy jacket and pants, with a salmon shirt beneath his blazer. His clothes had seen better days, and were worn at the elbows and knees, but they were certainly a step up from the dirty green graduation gown he once wore in the jungle. Remy wore his uniform with pride, and- at my insistence- kept his fingernails clipped.

Tonight he focused his resentment on being given the job of 'food taster.' I could see why Remy would be unhappy; after all, Odette was known for using poisons and powders. I wondered if she carried them hidden in her macoute. Of course, there was no way she would resort to such methods this evening, but in any case, a food taster would reassure the guests, and someone had to do it. Besides, this was an official function, so having a food taster gave the affair a more formal feeling. In addition, I would be the only one in the room commanding a subordinate, and this would elevate my standing among the rest; but to pull it off and create the right impression, I needed Remy's cooperation.

He poured cold water into the glasses of the guests. When he came to me, he overfilled mine, sloshing some onto the white tablecloth.

I pursed my lips in frustration. "Remy, you filled my glass to the brim. It's too much. It will spill as soon as I touch it. Some cold water would be nice. Please take it away and bring me half a glass." I meant to affect a sweet carefree tone, but I could not keep the underlying tension out of my voice. I knew I sounded like a harridan. I had to resist the urge to bite my fist.

Remy gave a slight bow, an even slighter smile, and raised one eyebrow. I knew that look! Damn the man! He waddled from the room with an air of injured dignity, and I distracted myself with small talk, inquiring how the guests fared on the journey to

Colombe Habitation, what they thought of the damp weather, and so on.

Joule was in good spirits. His clothing was a bit rumpled- both his white shirt and black slacks needed pressing- but in spite of that, he laughed easily in a booming voice. Joule controlled the amber trade. He was pragmatic, calculating, and ruthless, and although he did not look it, he could also be physically dangerous.

General Swain, on the other hand, was a relative newcomer to the political scene. The Doctor and I first met the General back at that infamous negotiation. Odette had been there too. Swain came from the Fraternité Internationale des Ouvriers en Electricité, better known as the FIOE, and was second-in-command of the opposing alliance. For the most part, he kept to himself, and spoke in a clipped staccato style. His military bearing gave him a dignity which Joule did not bother to affect. That told me Joule was confident, and this newcomer harbored a fundamental insecurity.

The lawyer, Burnette, was much the same as when I had last seen him, back in Ambreville. Burnette dressed with a sense of style, wearing a casual camel jacket, white shirt, and creased tan slacks. His attitude insinuated he was our superior and the rest of us were simply not up to his professional standards. Burnette controlled the law and the widely feared Ambreville police. For all his polish and refinement, he was nevertheless every bit as ruthless as Joule.

The one who really scared me was Odette. She was not much bigger than a child, with big brown eyes and ginger hair. Instead of the usual saffron ensemble, tonight the barefoot witch wore a dark brown dress. The effect was quite fetching in a nature-child kind of way, and men would fall all over themselves for one of her smiles, but I just couldn't understand a woman who did not like shoes. In any case, her specialties made her even more dangerous than the men.

Remy returned and placed a glass of water in front of me. The glass was literally cut in half, and then filled to the rim again.

The guests laughed, and I had to laugh too. "Picture the glass half broke," I said. There was a pause as everyone realized I had muffed the saying, and then all at once, more laughter, making me even more flustered.

"That's not how it goes!" Burnette said.

"Oh, never mind," Joule said with a good-natured wave of the hand.

"An optimist says the glass is half full," Burnette continued, "and a pessimist says it is half empty."

"I am an idealist," The Doctor declared. "The water is invisible, but I still believe the glass is full."

"Lift your glass," General Swain said, "and the water will spill, and the servant will have to clean up after your idealism."

Remy snorted when he heard the word 'servant.'

After more small talk, I regained my composure. "Remy," I said with a tight smile, "please uncover the serving dish for our guests."

He lifted the lid with a decided lack of enthusiasm. A cloud of steam rose from the dish, momentarily obscuring the course from view. I maintained my smile as the steam dissipated and observed my guests as they assimilated its import.

The lawyer drew a loud breath. General Swain straightened in his chair, apparently pleased with the selection. Joule adjusted his girth and rubbed his hands together in anticipation. I could not tell if Joule was oblivious to the symbolism, or simply did not care. He stroked his mustache in anticipation, and it was curiously revolting. Odette fumed. The Doctor looked profoundly unhappy. Whoever said revenge was a dish best served cold? I resisted the urge to laugh.

One or more of us would establish political dominance once and for all. General Swain possessed military strength, at least among the notoriously disorganized Fraternité Internationale des Ouvriers en Electricité, a group supposedly representing workers. Joule depended on the amber trade for his wealth, and mercenaries. The lawyer controlled the legal system and the Ambreville Police. The Doctor fronted the

Feux Follets cult. Odette nominally led the Children's Fund, but it was a shadow of its former self after the negotiation. She was simply too terrifying to even consider working with. All except Odette would consider allying with me, since I offered them legitimacy in the eyes of Nouveau Haitians, due to my position as The Official Hostess and my popularity among the poor.

I stared out the window while waiting for the others to be served. Across a ragged lawn of blue-green euphonia grass stood a flagpole, its flag- the flag of a defunct faction, the LAR- flying at half mast. We were close enough to the ocean for Colombe Habitation to experience the low marine layer and a lot of drizzle. In the last light of the evening's mist, a flock of scarlet mock mynahs appeared. They wheeled around the flagpole, flying as if they were one organism; next, they flew directly towards Colombe Habitation- and me- with manic energy, madly and loudly calling my name just as the original Grand Maestro, Alihak, had once taught them:

Vic-toooooor-iaaa

They flew over the house, circled, and flew back towards the pole and the dunes beyond. Past the dunes, low gray waves rolled across the oily alien ocean, slowly swelling and subsiding against the pebbled shore. Thinking of my pearls, I put water on them again. I glanced at Remy and gave him a slight nod, signaling him to serve the appetizer.

After a cursory taste, Remy placed a serving before Joule. The magnate began eating without waiting for the others. Remy did the same for General Swain, Burnette, and Odette.

"This is delicious, simply delicious." Joule slurped some gravy from a spoon.

"Look, it's so tender, the meat practically falls off the bone," General Swain added.

The lawyer looked pale, and for once, said nothing.

Odette pretended her serving did not exist.

Now Remy stood behind The Doctor. "Sir, would you like an appetizer?"

"No thank you," he answered, refusing to look my servant in the eye.

"Have one," Remy insisted. He stood ramrod straight and mustered as much dignity as he could, given his short stature; unfortunately, his erect posture made his ample stomach seem to protrude even more than usual. I covered my mouth with my hand.

"What's wrong?" Joule asked.

"You must not insult the Official Hostess," General Swain said.

"I am a vegetarian," Odette said, not bothering to conceal her irritation.

"I am a vegetarian, too," The Doctor stated. Odette might have been telling the truth about being a vegetarian, but I was pretty sure The Doctor was not, based on past experience; nevertheless, I had to admit, he looked ill, and it served him right. He stared with dismay at his plate and the small, pathetic carcasses curled upon it. "I am sorry, but I cannot eat this." He could not even bring himself to name it.

183

"No?" I asked in a tone of false sympathy. "Very well." I waved to Remy and he removed Odette's plate as well as The Doctor's dish. "They are just appetizers. Let's proceed to the main dish, shall we?"

"Excellent!" Joule exclaimed. General Swain agreed.

"What are we having?" the lawyer asked, shifting in his chair.

I smiled. "I am having a salad, heart of cycad with cayenne pepper, and caramelized ginger for dessert. So is Odette. There is only enough for the two of us. The rest of you are having spare ribs."

THE LIBRARY

After dinner we retired to the library. I waited for everyone else to go in and find their place. Most sank into plush chairs made of soft fabrics in various shades of red: cherry, coral, carmine, and rose. While they digested their meals, Burnette ranged around the room. After waiting a short time, I came in. *It is always important to make an entrance*, I thought. *Be memorable*. With head held high and shoulders rolled back, I made brief eye contact with each guest, smiled, and then followed Burnette at a respectful distance. "My compliments, Victoria," he said as he examined the full bookshelves lining the walls, running his long pale fingers along the spines of some of the tomes. "It is a fine collection, but there are no law books."

"Correct. What would be the point?" I asked.

"Nothing matters more than law," he said self-importantly.

General Swain laughed.

"You have your military laws too," Burnette said to General Swain. "You have rules of engagement, a code of conduct, and a system of military justice."

"Nice sentiments, lawyer, but meaningless in the field. Might makes right. Only action counts. But make up your stories about law if it makes you feel better. Go ahead. Write entire books. Fill whole bookshelves with them. It doesn't matter. Writing does not make them real." General Swain smirked. "Justice just is not. Justice is for 'just us.'"

Odette made a sour expression, folded her arms, and sank deeper into her chair. I think she was illiterate. I'm sure she hated Swain and The Doctor, because those two betrayed her father at that negotiation. I was there too, and so was Remy, but I doubted she held that against either of us, because we did not participate in the betrayal; and since my disapproval of The Doctor resulted in my exile, Odette might view me more favorably than I originally thought. The Doctor sat back and stared at the wooden ceiling as if he were remembering.

Joule laughed at Swain's jest. "Very clever, sir, very clever; but surely it is obvious the lawyer is correct. Contracts are a form of law. In a way, they make law possible in the first place. We depend on contracts to conduct business. We depend on them to trade amber. We depend on them to keep agreements." Joule briefly looked at General Swain and Odette. He did not look me in the eye. "So you see," Joule finished, "the lawyer has a point!"

"The point escapes me," General Swain said in a clipped staccato. "We do what is expedient. Laws are make-believe. Like books, they are a fiction. You know the old saying: 'history is written by the winner.' Laws and contracts exist to justify the results. It's entertaining. It makes everyone feel better about what happens." He put his hand to his chin, which prominently displayed his ring. It was made of rare blue amber, and contained a small, blue, eight-legged beetle frozen in time.

"Nice ring," Joule said, stroking his mustache. He was in the amber business. He could scarcely take his eyes off the gem.

"I detest bugs," General Swain said. "I detest beetles. I detest all creatures with eight legs."

"That is because you are afraid of them," Odette observed from the depths of her cushioned chair.

"You have a phobia," Burnette added.

"If it were up to me, I would exterminate the brutes-every beetle and spider and cycad hopper."

"*Tres charmant*," Odette said in a dry tone. Odette worried me. Having her and General Swain under the same roof was extremely dangerous- for him.

As for me, I remembered the eight legged fireflies hovering over yellow spear grass at twilight near Bois Caiman, their blue lights beckoning to potential hosts. I touched my pearls and avoided looking at General Swain.

Did The Doctor remember those fireflies? He cleared his throat and spoke. "I agree with Burnette. Law matters more because it is based upon consistent principles, rather than expediency. Nothing is more important than law, as long as the law is based upon loyalty and compassion."

I stood next to Burnette, lightly holding a bookshelf as if seeking support. From the corner of my eye, I gauged where the others might stand. Ever the professional, Burnette did not react, but since the statement by The Doctor should have received a favorable reaction, I had to assume the lawyer would not work with him. When they first arrived, Burnette and The Doctor indicated they had met before, but the lack of warmth suggested something had not gone well with their previous encounter. There seemed little chance of an alliance there. Joule, the tycoon, nodded slightly and folded his beefy hands in his lap. Again, his lack of reaction betrayed his true position. He should have agreed. He did not. Clearly, he would treat The Doctor as he treated other competitors, and find a way to eliminate him. General Swain narrowed his eyes and gave a predatory smile. He had been at odds with The Doctor from the very beginning. My guards and the traditional neutrality of Colombe Habitation might not be enough to protect The Doctor if General Swain decided to make this personal.

"Is it true," The Doctor asked me, "you have read every one of these books?"

"*Oui.* I am an avid reader."

"I find books useful," Joule interjected from the depths of his chair, "very useful indeed."

This surprised me, coming from Joule.

"Once," he continued, "a storm knocked down part of the wall in one of my stalls at the Amber Exchange. I used books to replace the wall. They did a fine job of keeping out the wind and rain while they lasted."

The lawyer ran his fingers across the book spines and read a few titles aloud: *"Circular Life... Colonialism, Then and Now... Consequences of Geographic Determinism upon Human Life and the Life Forms of Nouveau Haitiah... Convergent Evolution... The Fountain of Youth... The Myth of the Yew..."*

"Do you know why our world is called 'Nouveau Haitiah?" I asked. "Some colonists were from France and Haiti. We are becoming a 'new' form of Haitian."

"So," Burnette asked, "why should I care?"

"You should care," I said, fingering my pearls, "for your own good. You should learn more about your own world, and seek to live with it and understand it, rather than dominate and control it. How typically male! There is a better way for everyone."

"True!" Odette piped in.

"Men always want to control and dominate the native ecosystem," I continued. "They think the native flora and fauna are a means to an end; but they are an end in themselves. They are not a problem. They are a solution!"

Joule shook his head. "Poor dear, you shouldn't worry your pretty head about such things." General Swain sniggered.

"Solution?" Odette asked incredulously. "Nature is poisonous. At its heart, the world is toxic. I could tell you things about it that you would never, ever be able to forget. I saw the terrible truth of this in my own home town, Last Call. Have you ever heard of a yew?"

The Doctor asked Odette about it. At the same time, Joule made a foolish pun with the word 'yew.' General Swain and the lawyer laughed. I tried to speak, but they were all ignoring me. I refused to let them upset me, so I raised my voice and talked over them. "The best solution involves mutuality, shared dependence, and most of all, compassion; and that, gentlemen, is why I am the Official Hostess."

General Swain threw up his hands. "Another loud mouthed woman with an opinion!"

Odette swore at him.

"Drivel." Burnette gave me dismissive wave of the hand. "Obviously you are not a professional."

"Say, Burnette," Joule said. "What is the difference between a rooster and a lawyer?"

"What?"

"A rooster clucks defiance!" Joule laughed heartily at his own joke. Everyone else joined him, including me.

"I don't get it," Remy said.

The Doctor motioned Remy over to his chair. "Remy, switch the 'cl' in 'clucks' with the 'f' in 'defiance, and say it out loud."

Remy mumbled under his breath, and then laughed, slapping his knees.

Burnette's face reddened, but he pretended to ignore it. He pulled a large, heavy text from a shelf. "Here is an old one. The title has faded. What is this book, Victoria?"

"My grimoire."

"Grimoire?"

"My book of magic spells."

Burnette nearly dropped it. I crossed my arms and laughed to myself while he riffled through the pages, shaking his head. For the first time, Odette sat up and perched on the edge of her chair. The reference to magic caught her attention. "I know about your reputation," Burnette said to me. "It means nothing to me. I do not believe in magic." Odette smirked. Burnette really did not know who he was dealing with here. He underestimated me and he underestimated her. "By the way," he continued, "this is nothing but a textbook on Nouveau Haitian sea life."

"Right."

"Ugh. This thing is criminally ugly. What is it?" He showed me a dog-eared page with a lurid picture depicting a pale, bloated sea creature with undersized fins. The snouty head, with its tiny black eyes, tusks, and whiskers, appeared too small for its flabby, spotted body.

I smiled at Burnette. "That is one of my favorites, an adult sea swine. Its life cycle is fascinating. The adult's egg sacs-"

"That is disgusting," Burnette said abruptly, dropping the text on a nearby table. "I do not care about disgusting forms of sea life, and I do not care about useless books. We are gathered here tonight for a reason. We need to decide how our people will be ruled. Our people need law. They need order."

General Swain straightened in his chair. "Whose law, Lawyer? Whose order?"

"I have a name, Swain. It's Burnette."

"What we need," Joule said, talking over both of them, "is the magic of the marketplace. Markets provide the most efficient solutions. Let the largest, most profitable firms restore the economy, the amber trade, and peace."

General Swain leaned towards the heavy-set businessman and fired off words in short, rapid bursts. "Big businesses like your syndicate just redistribute wealth from the poor to the rich. There is not much to redistribute in the first place. That is because there is no order. There is no order because there is no hierarchy. We need order. We need hierarchy. That is what I bring to the table."

"That just kills young men in uniform," Joule said. The lawyer, doctor, and I nodded agreement.

"Not exactly." General Swain smiled. "Since I blame the business community for most of our problems, I prefer to target them. One corpse in a suit is worth twenty in uniform."

"Well, I never..." Joule's face turned red as he spluttered his indignation.

"Butcher," Burnette said.

"A butcher is an honest man," General Swain countered. "Like the butcher, I do my own work. You, however, are a hypocrite. You hide behind words. You hide behind books. You arrange for others to do your stealing and killing, and then you self-righteously proclaim 'the law' is on your side. You inflict taxation and imprisonment and capital punishment without even having the decency to blush."

"That reminds me," Joule said, leaning towards General Swain. "What do you have when you have a lawyer buried up to his neck in black sand?"

"What?"

"Not enough sand."

While the guests continued trading barbs, I assessed my options. At any place other than Colombe Habitation, the political question would have been resolved quickly and violently. Here, negotiated settlement was possible. My being there helped, since the men tended to modify their aggressive behavior in the presence of an attractive woman. How they viewed Odette was a mystery to me- I think they basically feared her; on the one hand, although she had the unmistakable figure of a woman, she looked like a child; on the other hand, she was weird and incomprehensible, at least to me. The Doctor and Swain would never ally with her. Burnette severely underestimated her. Joule would be her best bet. Still, I was uncertain if any of them would even ally with each other. The bigger problem was that none of them seemed interested in allying with me, and I did not have the resources to stand alone. Burnette seemed like my best option. Between the two of us, we would have the power, political connections, wealth, and popularity to rule. The Doctor came in a distant second. His power relied on the cult of Feux Follets, and he had few connections and little wealth. The matter remained up in the air, and to me, that was unacceptable. I needed to secure my position as The Official Hostess. I *would* secure it. But how?

"Look!" The Doctor said with pleasure, "Professor Alihak's *Redeeming Time and Memory*. I knew him well." The Doctor then noticed another thick tome on one shelf, smiled, and turned to me. "And here is *A La Recherche du Temps Perdu- A Remembrance of Things Past*. Do you read Proust?"

"*Oui*." I wanted to change the subject, but he was becoming enthused.

"I wrote my University thesis on Proust and his life."
He reached for *A La Recherche du Temps Perdu.* I
could not let that happen.

"He was born in Auteuil and died in Lutetia Hospital-"
he continued.

In another moment he would attempt to pull the book
from the shelf, but that would cause a big problem,
because it was a prop, and not a real book. I
consciously projected my voice to address the group
and draw his attention away from it. "Perhaps we
should address the reason we are here. Perhaps a
negotiated settlement is possible."

The Doctor turned away from the bookshelf and
agreed. Upon hearing the phrase 'negotiated
settlement' Odette covered her mouth and laughed to
herself.

"I heard what happened on the Phosphor Plain the
last time you conducted a negotiation, Doctor" Joule
said with a twinkle in his eye. I had been present too,
but I was not about to draw attention to that fact.
The atmosphere of my soiree- and the topic of
conversation- needed to change again immediately.

While the others talked, I signaled Remy to bring the after-dinner liqueur.

"I remember that negotiation too," General Swain said. "I am no Lord Waterman or Commissar Ampere."

"It's about time you and I had a talk, don't you think?" Odette said in a high, tight voice while patting the macoute by her side. It was strange, because she was not addressing anyone in the room. I was sure she was talking to her macoute, or perhaps something inside it. She smiled at me, but her hazel eyes showed no emotion whatsoever. Was she some sort of a sociopath?

"Why should any of us negotiate away their strength?" Joule asked The Doctor. "I have my mercenaries. General Swain has the FIOE, a small but formidable force. Odette commands what is left of the Children's Fund. Burnette has his death squads- I mean, the Ambreville Police. Even you have your followers."

"Like Victoria, I do not rely on armies," The Doctor replied a bit self-righteously. He was being hypocritical; after all, his followers were the Feux Follets, a fanatical cult devoted to him. "We can all find a mutually satisfying outcome if use we use logic and reason," he continued. "We can work together."

"In its very nature the world is like the law: adversarial," the lawyer pronounced.

"Not if you practice compassion," The Doctor countered.

"I do not accept plea bargains," Burnette retorted, "so do not attempt to play upon my emotions."

General Swain tilted his head and smiled, revealing large, yellow teeth. "All decisions are emotional decisions," he said. "Decisions are usually made instantly, within moments of facing a choice. They are made based on emotions. Everything that follows is just a rationalization to confirm it. Reason and logic are used to confirm an irrational choice. Compassion is a fool's emotion."

"It is not an emotion," The Doctor said.

"It is more than an emotion," I said at the same time.

"Empathy and compassion are inadequate responses to death and social anarchy," Burnette stated in a prim, flat tone, and if he had practiced repeating the line to himself.

Remy entered the library and the conversation stopped. He was carrying a circular tray of shot glasses and a large black bottle of diamond root liqueur. In its distilled form, the liqueur was a mild stimulant and hallucinogen. Judging from the bounce in his step and the brightness of his dilated eyes, the servant had already performed his food tasting duties without being asked. He distributed the shot glasses with uncharacteristic enthusiasm.

"A toast!" Joule said. "I would like to propose a toast!"

"What are we toasting?" Burnette asked.

"Why, Nouveau Haitiah!" Joule raised his shot glass.

"To good health," The Doctor added.

"*A votre Sante*," I echoed along with the others. I inspected the thick black liquid and sniffed its aroma with a connoisseur's appreciation. It tickled my nose with the odor of anise and old campfire. I raised the shot glass to my lips, closed my eyes, and took a small sip. The sweet, oily, ashen flavor of the drink oozed over my tongue and down my throat, filling my midsection with an expanding, blossoming heat. Ah, diamond root liqueur.

Burnette raised his glass. "I would like to propose another toast: To the Official Hostess of Nouveau Haitiah."

"To the Unofficial-" General Swain started to say, lifting his shot glass towards Odette.

"To the Official Hostess," The Doctor loudly proclaimed, drowning out General Swain, and he tossed down his drink.

I drained my glass and set it down harder than I had intended. Willing my fingers to stop trembling, I steadied my hand, dipped it in the nearby bowl of sea water, and touched my pearls. I must not show weakness! After the lawyer toasted me, General Swain had the unmitigated nerve to insult the heart of my power! Even worse, he started to refer to that odious Odette as 'The Unofficial Hostess'! And to make it even more galling, if possible, the only thing that saved me was the Doctor, of all people, talking over General Swain!

How could they do this to me? All I ever wanted to do was make a difference, a positive difference- ease suffering, help the poor, donate to charities, and improve the lot of women and children. If it required me to project an image that included fabulous clothes and stylish shoes, was that so wrong?

Loud laughter interrupted my reverie. The faces of the lawyer and general shone with an almost imperceptible glow, and instead of carefully enunciating each word, the lawyer was beginning to slur, a sure sign the narcotic drink was taking effect. The Doctor stared into his half-full shot glass with a crooked smile, as if sympathizing with his own memories.

"Play some music," Odette said, swaying in her seat. "I feel like dancing."

Remy came to stand by the side of her chair and stared at her small bare feet. He self-consciously brushed the front of his salmon shirt, and then refilled her shot glass without being asked. His big eyes were dilated, his movements crisp and precise. Odette drained her shot in one gulp.

"Would you like to dance?" Remy asked with all the gallantry he could muster. The fool was completely infatuated with her. Blame it on diamond root.

"No. To dance, we need music," she replied. "Ask the Grand Maestro over there," she said, tossing her head in the direction of The Doctor. The Doctor shook his head and threw up his hands in a warding gesture.

"Another toast," the lawyer said, his sweeping gesture encompassing all in expansive good will. "To Victoria, for the fine meal-"

"- And drink," Joule laughed.

"- And talk of beetles and Sea Swine," General Swain finished. I raised a brow at that comment. Clearly, General Swain had no idea what he was toasting. I reached for a bowl of sea water in order to wet my pearls again, but none was at hand. It had been too long since I had touched them, and they were drying out and losing their nacreous luster, and that was not good. From the corner of my eye I observed The Doctor hesitating to raise his glass. He was literate and knowledgeable. Did he know that knowledge was the real source of my power? Did the comment about Sea Swine mean anything to him? The Doctor's eyes narrowed, and much to my surprise, he shrugged and smile.

"Especially Sea Swine!" he said, and in one motion, tossed down his glass of liqueur.

205

THE COUP

The gathering broke up late. I escorted my guests up the spiral flight of stairs to their sleeping quarters, and directed Remy to take care of security. He wanted to post my Colombe Habitation guards at the door of each guest's room, with Remy personally standing guard outside my door. It seemed excessive, and the chances of Remy successfully defending me from anything seemed remote, to say the least, but I went along with it.

Entering my room, I closed the heavy wooden door and undressed. I donned a black nightgown, little more than a slip, and sat before my vanity table mirror. I removed my black diamond earrings and set them next to the coral and aquamarine colored jewelry box. A black crystal ball occupied one corner of my table, and my personal shrine the other. The shrine consisted of a small globe, a miniature vanity mirror, and a pair of amber dice. Later I would fix my meditations upon them. For now, sitting bare armed before the mirror, I picked up my brush and proceeded to comb it through my thick black hair, running the fingers of my free hand through it after each stroke, and then brushing again. Stroke after stroke, I brushed with an unfocused stare, reflecting on recent events. The longer I stared, the more the mirror came to resemble a pond, a round pool of boundless depth and timelessness. *'The soul migrates to water,'* I thought, as my image seemingly swam in its watery depths, a confirmation of my own reflected vanity. Just as a flowing fountain causes a pool to overflow and cascade from basin to basin, to ultimately return and flow again, so my brushstrokes fed my meditations upon my own reflection, and so my reflection fed my boundless vanity. I passed my time in my bedroom like people pass their years, absorbed in myself, yet ignored by the world outside my heavy wooden door; however, the world was not done with me just yet. Before I could finish my bedtime routine, remove my make-up, and take off my Nouveau Haitian pearl necklace and place it in its bowl of sea water, a commotion filled the hallway.

Heavy boots pounded up the stairs. Confused roars of challenge and command reverberated through the wing; enraged shouts and cries of pain filled Colombe Habitation, followed by more heavy footsteps in the hallway outside my door.

My bedroom door banged from an impact. I recognized the sound of a body hitting it, followed by a slide down to the threshold. A familiar voice moaned my name.

"Victoria. Help me."

Remy! He was hurt! Anger filled my heart. How dare they assault my personal servant! Someone was violating the neutrality of Colombe Habitation, violating my home, and violating the hospitality of The Official Hostess of Nouveau Haitiah. That was unforgivable; but to harm someone as defenseless and feckless as Remy was beyond contempt.

Voices in the hallway barely registered with me as I strode to the door. I turned the doorknob, and jumped back when it opened into the room faster than I expected. The weight of my servant, Remy, who had been resting against the door in a sitting position, pushed it inward. He slumped backward onto the floor, a thin red trickle flowing from one ear, and it stained the collar of his salmon colored shirt.

I dragged him over the threshold and checked his pulse. It was weak, but at least he was still alive. "Someone will pay for this, Remy," I swore. More cries and moans of pain came from outside my door. Enraged, I entered the hallway without thinking about the danger.

General Swain stood at the other end of the hallway, surrounded by several of his soldiers. They wore dun fatigues with black splotches.

"The guards?" General Swain asked.

One soldier waved a bloody machete. "Done, sir."

I marched down the hallway, past the bodies of my guards. The knot of men failed to notice me.

"Were any guards taken prisoner?"

"No, sir."

"Good."

"General, the grounds are secured," another soldier reported.

"Well done. Bring me the captives."

As I approached, more soldiers entered the hallway from another room. They escorted three prisoners: Joule, The Doctor, and Burnette. One soldier stood by the businessman, who seemed calm. The Doctor offered no resistance, but two soldiers shoved him against the wall anyway. Four others carried Burnette by his arms and legs. The lawyer struggled frantically, twisting and kicking, but the soldiers maintained their grip.

I pushed my way through the soldiers. They gaped, and their eyes widened as surprise gave way to superstitious fear. None of them had ever faced the full fury of a reputed witch. I stood straight, my eyes blazing. I forgot all about being short, or the fact that I was barefoot and wearing only a black slip and a pearl necklace while confronting armed killers.

"General, how dare you! As Official Hostess-"

His fist caught me in the solar plexus, lifting me off my feet and knocking the wind out of me. I fell to my hands and knees, gasping for breath, my black hair forming a curtain around my face. General Swain turned from me to address Joule.

"Your mercenaries betrayed you. They surrendered to my army without a fight. Now they work for me."

"I see." Joule looked down, slowly shaking his head. Even his mustache seemed to droop. "They didn't stay bought. I guess I shouldn't be surprised."

"They will give me the edge I need to mop up Burnette's death squads. Joule, I can still use your support network and your financial backing. From now on, you work for me too. Agreed?"

Joule shrugged and then smiled. "All things considered, I would be glad to accept the offer."

"Good. Where is the witch Odette? Does anyone know?"

"She was not in her room," one soldier answered. The other soldiers shook their heads and murmured among themselves. No one knew if she had escaped. The General narrowed his eyes to slits. "Not good," he muttered through clenched teeth, and then shouted in anger, and pounded the hallway wall with his open hand.

Four soldiers still held Burnette by his limbs, a few inches off the floor. Burnette calmed down enough to stop struggling, and listen to the deal made between General Swain and the tycoon. He remained silent as Swain walked over to him. The General towered over him, polished jack boots next to the lawyer's head. "I won, lawyer. You lost. Case closed."

"No!" Burnette jerked and twisted and turned as hard as he could. The soldiers fought to maintain their hold. "Wait! You can't do this! I know secrets. I know valuable information."

"Go on," he said evenly.

"Information about Auteuil- I... I know the cause of the Fièvre Pourpre outbreak."

General Swain curled his lip. "The Doctor can fill me in about that. What else?" Other soldiers surrounded the lawyer, drawing their machetes.

"You betrayed me!" Burnette was hyperventilating.

General Swain shrugged. "Kill the lawyer. No need to be neat."

He turned from the lawyer and faced me. Burnette begged for his life, saying "no, please," over and over. General Swain started to say something to me, but the lawyer's screams grew louder and shriller, and the soldiers laughed raucously. The soldiers had tied Burnette's ankles together and hung him upside down from a ceiling beam, like a pig to be slaughtered. General Swain made a quick slicing motion with his palm across his throat. A gout of blood splashed on the floor, and I closed my eyes.

General Swain struck a pose, hands on hips. "So that is how an intelligent creature behaves in its dying moment!"

I cursed him.

"Silence, witch. Your turn. Let's see you manage the moment." General Swain lunged towards me. His assault made the other soldiers forget their fear, and they converged on me. One reached for my shoulder, and I allowed his hand to slip under the strand of my necklace. At the same time, General Swain drew back his arm and gave me a tremendous slap across my face. The blow jerked my head sideways, away from the soldier grasping my necklace. He lost his grip, but the necklace broke. Now, one loose strand draped across my collar bone. I grasped the loose end and whirled it over my head, slinging pearls against the wall. They clattered and rolled in every direction, initiating a mad scramble amongst the soldiers. Even Joule and General Swain chased the rolling pearls, climbing over one another in their greed to pocket some for themselves.

I stood, motionless and silent and smiling in disdain, while the troops argued among about the division of their ill-gotten gains. To my surprise, The Doctor also stood nearby, motionless and silent. Unlike the others, he had not participated in the scramble for my Nouveau Haitian pearls.

General Swain resolved the arguments by ensuring each soldier received at least one pearl. Several clamored for more treasure, and asked to ransack the premises. General Swain assented. Chaos ensued.

Soldiers entered my room, and came out carrying my clothes, shoes, and jewelry box. Two of them dragged my dazed servant Remy into the hallway, and left the heavy man sitting in front of their leader. General Swain frowned. "What did you find besides a useless fat man?"

"No weapons, no amber, and no liqueur," one reported.

"I found a pair of black diamond ear rings in this jewelry box," added another.

"Any sign of Odette?"

"No sir. The two men who were guarding her room are dead. Their faces are covered with yellow powder. Another was killed with a machete near the front entrance."

General Swain pursed his lips and stared into the distance. "She must have escaped. We cannot follow her into the jungle. There are not enough of us, and she is too dangerous." He grimaced and came to a decision. "Let her go." He sighed and shook his head. "This is not good. Now we will have to deal with her another time." General Swain turned to me. "Where is your safe?"

I raised my chin and said nothing.

"Where do you keep your valuables?" This time, when I refused to speak, he slapped me.

"Sir, what shall we do with this prisoner?" one of the soldiers standing by Remy asked. He drew his machete, making his preference clear. Another drew his machete and closed on The Doctor, who kept a straight posture while staring at the floor.

Remy struggled feebly. "Victoria," he pleaded.

"Well, witch?" General Swain said, "where is your safe?"

"I will tell you if you spare Remy and The Doctor."

General Swain smiled. "All right."

I did not believe he would keep his word- at least, not for long- but what choice did I have? "Remy, show them my safe. Also, open my black diamond liqueur cabinets to them."

A cheer erupted from the soldiers. General Swain raised his hand. "Tonight, we celebrate. We will reap our rewards and our well-earned trophies. You," he said, gesturing to two soldiers, "confine the witch and The Doctor to her room."

The soldiers looked crestfallen at the prospect of missing out on the looting.

"Do not worry. You will be rewarded in the morning for doing your duty." He glanced in my direction, and returned his attention to the two soldiers. "Believe me; she will be worth the wait."

IN MY ROOM

I closed my bedroom door, leaned against it, and sighed. My vanity table was empty now. The looters had taken the globe, mirror and dice from my shrine, along with my coral and aquamarine jewelry box. The crystal ball lay on the floor in one corner.

The Doctor paced the length of the room. He walked to a large paned window and looked down at the flagstones below. "Is there another way out of here?"

"Of course not! This is my bedroom. I sleep here. What did you expect, some sort of secret passage?"

He pointed to a door in the corner. "Where does that lead?"

"That's my closet."

He opened it, and his jaw dropped in exaggerated surprise. "Amazing."

"That's private, if you don't mind! What's so amazing about it?"

"The clothes! The shoes! How did you get so many?"

"Well, I am the Official Hostess of Nouveau Haitiah, you know."

"Yes, but I thought you gave everything to charity."

"Oh, come on. I have to project an image. People expect it. Besides, I like clothes, and I like shoes. What is wrong with that? Most of the shoes are old, anyway."

Shaking his head, he returned to the window and stared down, into the silver mist of the night. It did not take witchcraft to read his mind. "Forget it. It's too far down."

"Do you have any rope?"

"No." After a moment, the idea struck me as funny. "Rope in my bedroom? What kind of a girl do you think I am?"

He looked me in the eye. "It is no joke, you know. We need to find a way out of here. Maybe we could tie some sheets together. We have to escape. They will kill us in the morning."

"No they won't."

"Don't be naïve, Victoria. Your status will not save you. General Swain violated your home, your hospitality, and your person."

"I beg your pardon! That is not true! No one, but no one, violates my person. And I am not naïve."

That flustered him. "I mean, he slapped you. They took your pearls and Joule-"

"-You didn't take any, did you?"

"What? Your pearls? No, of course not. Listen to me. We are in great danger if we stay here. General Swain will not keep his end of the deal, and we both know it. He will have us executed in the morning. We have to get out tonight. Don't you understand? If we stay here, we will die."

I took a deep breath. "Look, I'm telling you, we're not going to die."

"Not if I can help it." From the hallway came the sound of laughing soldiers, and bodies being dragged down the corridor. He paced about my room. "Do you have any weapons?"

"That's not necessary," I replied. "Besides, this is my bedroom. I don't keep weapons in my bedroom." I looked him up and down. He was a good looking man, above average height and trim, but not what one would call physically intimidating. "Seriously, are you a fighter?"

"Hard to say." We both knew he was not. He smiled. "Are you a witch?"

We both laughed. After a few moments we lapsed into silence. The silence stretched long enough to make me self-conscious. Here I stood, face to face with a man in my bedroom, and I was wearing nothing more than a black slip. I blushed, but if he noticed, he had the grace to let it go. I liked him. He was respectful, resourceful, and educated. We were unwilling allies, but the prospect seemed more and more bearable, perhaps even appealing.

Finally I spoke. "I prefer to be known as The Official Hostess. I read, and I treasure knowledge. In the minds of some, that makes me a witch."

"Fair enough."

"I've heard you called The Doctor, Witch Doctor, Surgeon General, and even The Grand Maestro. I've heard wild stories about what happened after we parted at Bois Caiman; about how you spread La Fièvre Pourpre at Auteuil, and performed a ritual killing at Lutetia Hospital, and how you yourself were resurrected by the bank of the Bimi- well, we both know what happened there- and other weird stuff about zombies. Is any of it true?"

"Those stories come from the Feux Follets. I am not any of those things. I am like you. I am just a guy who likes to read books. I was hoping to do some good here."

I knew the truth behind what happened at Bois Caiman and the tale of Korpusant and his supposed resurrection, because I was there, so I was willing to take The Doctor's word about the other rumors. Another long pause followed. "What about your family?" I asked.

"I never really had a family," he replied. "Right now, Victoria, I have only you. Let us be true. Let us be true to one another."

"It's not that easy. Let me think about it."

"Don't think too long. We are running out of time."

I made a decision. "We have plenty of time. Let me explain."

REVENGE

The Doctor rested in the corner with his back against the wall, sitting with his legs crossed and in a meditative posture. I tossed and turned in my bed while raucous shouts and cheers came from the vicinity of the flagpole out front. At one point, I went to the window and peered into the night, but mist and darkness obscured the view. Sometime before dawn, the noise stopped, and I fell into a deep slumber.

I awoke with a start. Ghostly tapping filled my bedroom like the eerie rapping from a séance. Where did it come from? The window? The flagpole? The fog outside made it impossible to judge time of day, and the dim, diffuse quality of light made it seemed like my room was filled with Nouveau Haitian mist as well. How long had I slept? The tapping continued, more insistent now, and I realized someone was at my bedroom door. I gazed at The Doctor; he was awake now, and in answer to my unspoken question, he shrugged.

I cleared my throat. "Who's there?"

"It's me."

"Remy!" I ran to the door and flung it open. "You're alive! I'm so glad to see you!"

"I'm glad to see you too." He managed a weary smile. "I thought I was alone."

"Alone?" My heart jumped. "What do you mean? Where is the staff of Colombe Habitation- the cook, the maid, the gardener- all the others? And where are the soldiers?"

"I don't know. Last night, the soldiers made me show them the safe. I opened it for them. I showed them the liqueurs too, like you told me. They thought it would be funny to lock me in the pantry, and then they forgot about me and left me in there. They drank the entire stock of diamond root."

"*Bon*."

"That was a lot of diamond root liqueur." Remy shook his head in sorrow.

"*Oui*, I know. Then what happened."

"They looted Colombe Habitation. Those drunkards took everything, even the place settings. I can't believe how much noise they made!" Remy paused and looked down. "They killed the guards in the upstairs hallway, Victoria."

For a moment I choked up and could not speak. Finally I collected myself. "I know, Remy. I know."

Remy straightened and narrowed his eyes. "They violated the traditions of Colombe Habitation."

"You are lucky to be alive," The Doctor said.

Remy agreed and rubbed his head. "It still hurts. I can't believe they killed the guards. I knew those men."

"How did you escape?" The Doctor asked.

"What happened to the rest of my staff?" I asked at the same time.

"At first," Remy said, "I didn't want to leave the pantry. I heard them take away the Chef. I don't know what happened to the others. I was sure they would kill me, but they must have forgotten about me. Finally, it got quiet. I must have fallen asleep. When I woke up, there was no sound coming from outside, nothing. I figured the soldiers were either asleep or gone, so I came to find you."

"Maybe my staff took advantage of the mist to slip away."

The Doctor held up one finger. "Wait a minute. You said they locked you in the pantry! How did you get out?"

Remy smiled sheepishly. "A hidden tunnel connects the pantry with the library."

"You mean a secret passage?" The Doctor laughed, and I laughed with him.

"A simple lever operates the door inside the pantry," I explained. "Pulling out a thick book on a library bookshelf operates the other side. I actually saw you looking at it last night."

"What book?"

"*A La Recherche du Temps Perdu.*"

The Doctor tilted his head and gave me an odd look.

Remy looked at both of us as if we were out of our mind. "But what happened to the soldiers?"

"The place seems deserted," The Doctor observed.

"I think I know what happened to the soldiers," I said. "Come with me."

After a quick breakfast we changed into warm clothes. The men donned camel trench coats and canvas hats. I put on my taupe raincoat and carried my navy blue and salmon umbrella and led The Doctor and Remy outside. They walked on either side of me through the cold swirling mist, typical morning weather along the coast. Tiny beads of moisture dappled the skin of my face, forming drops like liquid pearls. The beads of water soon joined together and ran in little rivulets down my cheek and chin, and down to the hollow of my collar bone. Despite my warm clothing and umbrella, I was soon soaked to the skin, as were the two men.

We crossed the wet euphonia grass and headed towards the sound of the flagpole. The soft, rhythmic clanging of its pulley penetrated the foggy mist to guide us. The clanging seemed muffled compared to yesterday, but I thought that might be due to the moisture in the air.

We came across several items of navy and salmon colored clothing strewn on the ground. I feared the worst. At last, the flagpole's outline took shape in the mist. I could make out an amber and black flag atop the mast and I could make out the clanging pulley, but the rope looked wrong, as if it were threaded with a bunch of large, dark, oblong beads. If someone was making a pearl necklace, it was a poor job; the beads looked unbalanced, and the rope did not seem to run through all of the bead's centers. Some of the unevenly threaded beads appeared to trail strands of kelp. A few steps closer to the pole revealed the true nature of the beads: they were the heads of my butchered staff; the kelp, their hair; and the rope ran through their necks, exiting their mouths. General Swain and his soldiers had created a hideous mockery of my pearl necklace.

I cried. I cried in anguish, in sympathy, in anger, in dismay. These were the men and women who had lived with me at Colombe Habitation, and although I knew them well, their expressions were so disfigured by the pain of death as to be nearly unrecognizable. Disbelief, shock, and rage washed over me, but not acceptance, never that. My vengeance would be almost as terrible as these vile acts.

The Doctor stood by my side, dumbfounded by the gory spectacle. Remy quietly wept. I walked past the flagpole and examined the ground for telltale signs, and found what I expected: footprints made by heavy boots, heading for the ocean, and wide tracks of crushed grass showing heavy objects had been dragged. With one hand I made the sign of the crossroads. "We'll come back soon and attend to the bodies of my poor friends. Come with me. I want you to see this."

The two men followed me towards the sea. We entered the dunes, holding our umbrellas with one hand and extending the other arm to maintain our balance. The lawn of euphonia gave way to tussocks of spear grass. The trail of trampled footprints continued across the low dunes, and when the grass transitioned to sand, the heavy objects that were being dragged left furrows, making it easy to follow. In the distance, I detected the muffled pulse of the ocean, and the clicks and clatters of pebbles being tossed by the low waves on the long rocky shore. As we made our way, the footprints became progressively rarer, until at last they disappeared; yet shreds of torn clothing littered the trail, along with the occasional soldier's boot.

"Victoria," Remy asked, "where are we going?"

"The beach."

The low roar and gentle hiss of advancing and retreating waves grew louder, and the damp sand underfoot became interspersed with shelves of worn gray rock. We forged our way through the mist, following one deep furrow in particular. An eerie sound rose over the roar of the sea, a series of grunts and long groans, punctuated by high pitched, piggish squeals. More grunts and snorts answered from further down the beach.

"What is that?" The Doctor asked. "I have never heard anything like it."

"Me neither," Remy agreed. "It's not right. It's... unnatural. What do you think it is, Victoria?"

A loud, drawn-out squeal pierced the mist.

"That," I answered, "is the sound of my revenge."

Remy made a warding gesture with one pudgy hand. "Witchcraft!"

The Doctor's eyes widened. "What have you done?"

"See for yourself." They walked with me as I followed the deep furrow through the sand. At last, we came upon the track's creator: a large, mottled, writhing object. As we approached closer, the men recognized what I already suspected, that the thing in the sand was not an object at all, but a creature, squealing and heaving its enormous girth in an effort to reach the sea.

The creature paused in its furrow, gasping for breath. Cracks ran across its pale blotchy skin, revealing pink flesh beneath each crevice. When it became aware of my presence, it used its four limbs to twist and roll onto its back, exposing its pale pink stomach. With difficulty, the creature lifted its small, almost human-shaped head, snuffling the air as if seeking a scent. It found what is was looking for, and briefly locked its black beady eyes upon me.

The two men stood nearby. The Doctor spoke first. "I know this monster."

Remy agreed. "I could swear this monster has a face. See there! It looks like that businessman, Joule. That's his mustache, just beneath the snout!"

"You're right," I said. "That is Joule."

The creature's eyes darted in fear from me to The Doctor to Remy, with no sign of recognition. He- or it- gave an anguished squeal, followed by several snorts, but I could not tell whether Joule was communicating, or could even understand his condition. His body had swollen to twice its normal size and his belly was severely distended. Atrophied arms and legs had lost their fingers and toes; they now resembled half-formed fins, too weak to support his tremendous weight. In addition, his nose had lost its shape, and deteriorated into a boneless snout. Joule's ears hung limply, mere fleshy blobs, no longer giving even a hint of their original form or purpose.

The Doctor shook his umbrella and gathered himself. "You did this to him?"

"He did it to himself."

"Witchcraft, witchcraft, witchcraft," Remy muttered to himself.

"You turned him into a sea swine," The Doctor concluded.

I nodded. "The others, too. The soldiers deserved it. Joule deserved it. General Swain deserved it most of all. They murdered my people. They violated the sanctity of Colombe Habitation. They violated the basic tenets of hospitality. They were rude, they were violent, they mistreated Remy, they drank my liqueur and they stole my pearls. They were evil, and in every possible sense, they were untrue to me."

From up and down the rocky slate beach, a hideous chorus pierced the mist as the sea swine called back and forth. The creature that had been Joule rolled its eyes upwards and groaned feebly. It was having trouble breathing; its weight was crushing its lungs.

The Doctor wiped water from his eyes. The mist had turned to light rain. "How did you do it?"

"Witchcraft," Remy muttered. "Worse than zombies."

"Remember my pearls?"

The Doctor nodded. Remy stopped muttering when he heard the word 'pearls,' and stared at me.

"Those pearls," I continued, "are the egg sacs of sea swine. Nothing happens as long as they are kept moist with sea water. If they are warmed and dry out, they hatch. Since they are parasites, they immediately seek a host."

"So they hatched," The Doctor said. A wavelet rolled in, tumbling smooth rounded rocks in the surf. Joule chuffed and groaned, straining his swollen body in the direction of the ocean.

"That's right," I said, "they hatched. And they all kept the eggs on their persons, warm and dry. You know, Joule and General Swain and the soldiers never valued knowledge. They knew nothing of Nouveau Haitian sea life, or sea swine. The entire ecosystem is parasitic and interdependent, but instead of respecting its mutualism and learning about it, they either ignored it, or tried to ride roughshod over it."

"They only listened to their own greed," The Doctor added. He gave Remy a long look. Remy used to have a reputation for taking items that did not belong to him, and the LAR Quartermaster Faraday used to regularly curse him up one side and down the other for it, but that was a long time ago; I knew beyond any shadow of a doubt that Remy would never take anything of mine.

"Wait a minute! I thought the flora and fauna of Nouveau Haitiah generally left people alone," The Doctor said. "They might bite or sting or even shock, but that is about it. These sea swine actually tried to reproduce through their hosts."

I agreed. "It was caused by a fatal combination of desire and greed and ignorance. Diamond root and black diamonds are at the heart of the Nouveau Haitian ecosystem. They form the base of the system. They are the attractor that binds. And those men were besotted with diamond root liqueur."

"Ah. I see. It must have been oozing from their skin like an aphrodisiac."

"Exactly. The sea swine larvae work fast anyway, and the liqueur must have acted like a supercharger. The larvae anesthetized and penetrated the skin, then made for the lungs. From there, the infestation reproduced and multiplied like a virus; it spread at an exponential rate, and drove the host to seek the ocean."

The sea swine Joule breathed intermittent gulps of air, followed by wet choking coughs. Remy took a step closer to it. "Will he die?"

I nodded. "The ocean is close, but I doubt he will make it that far."

"What about General Swain and the other soldiers?"

"Hear those squeals? They will be dead soon too."

The Doctor wiped the rain from his face. "The soul migrates to water."

"It doesn't always make it there," I observed.

"We are soaking wet," The Doctor said. "Looks like the water is migrating to us."

Remy held out a hand. "It's raining harder."

"I'm cold." I wrapped my arms around myself and shivered. "These umbrellas aren't helping much. Let's go back to Colombe Habitation and get out of the rain."

Remy pointed at the surf. "What is that?" Not far offshore, an electrical glow came from under the surface.

"Must be white whips," I said. "I'm not going closer to find out. Let's go."

With that, we left the shore. The Doctor walked by my side. Remy trailed a few steps behind us.

"They were violent men," The Doctor said, "and they died violently. Nature killed them."

"There is natural violence, and there is violence between humans; one is not an excuse for the other."

"It is violence, just the same," The Doctor noted.

"True. Yet the natural cycle of Nouveau Haitiah only involves violence when the flora and fauna eat each other in order to reproduce. There is no cruelty to it. They are interdependent, every one of them; really, they are all versions of the same entity. But the violence between people is unnecessary and often cruel. We can overcome it. In a sense, we are all the same too. I am talking about simple compassion."

"Compassion conquers all," The Doctor said. He gave me a sidelong smile. "Don't you think we should be closer?"

"We're close enough, for now."

He took my hand. I let him hold it. "You realize," he said, "that we are now the undisputed rulers of Nouveau Haitiah. We won."

I laughed at him. "What do you mean, 'we'?"

"You and me," he said simply. Remy must not have heard us, because he remained silent.

"What about Odette?" I asked. "She is still out there."

"She cannot stop us."

"What makes you so sure? She is dangerous. She could kill us. She will surely try."

"Yes, but she has no political power. You have the support of Nouveau Haitians. I have the Feux Follets behind me. We will protect each other, and we can make good things happen. We will make great allies! Think of we can do!"

"Go on," I said, smiling encouragement.

"Let us be allies, Victoria. Let us be more than that. Let us be true to one another."

"I'm willing," I said, and, I have to admit it, I laughed with pleasure.

Remy loudly cleared his throat. "I will continue to monitor and act in your best interests, as befits my new title."

"Oh really?" I said. "What is your new title?"

"Aide-de-camp," he declared. "And I will be true to both of you too, even though I am certain you are a witch."

"You are a witch," The Doctor echoed.

"That sounds so superstitious. What I am, gentlemen, is the Official Hostess of Nouveau Haitiah."

CODA

"Where are you?"

"In here, Victoria."

The bathroom door creaked when I opened it, and my coral hued high heels clacked upon the bathroom's blue tile floor. I wore my dove grey dress with an aquamarine sash, and strode across the floor the same way as I would any other, with shoulders back and posture erect; after all, impressions always matter, even with old friends. Many years had passed since that memorable night at Colombe Habitation, when The Doctor and I more or less conquered the world, or at any rate, were the last political players left standing (with the exception of Odette- but more about her later). Through political power we had achieved many of our hopes and dreams and done many good things, and yet all had not gone well for The Doctor.

Although the bathroom on this second floor of Government House was dimly lit, I could see The

Doctor wore nothing at all; he was resting naked in an empty, stand-alone bathtub. He put his book down on his lap, and draped one arm over the edge of the tub. An empty glass of water stood upon the tile floor. He idly rubbed the rim.

"Victoria. It has been a long time," he said. "Come closer."

I stood still. He was obviously depressed, but this was simply rude and, old friends or not, no way to treat a lady, never mind the Official Hostess. I was so mad I did not even bother with small talk. "What are your plans?" Inwardly I winced, because I do not like using that demanding tone, but when he failed to respond, I grew angrier. If there is one thing I will not stand for, it is being ignored. I repeated my question- and I was loud. At least that got a stir out of him.

"Stop! Don't you dare judge. I am wealthy. I am powerful. On balance, I have done well. So have you." He reached for the tap and idly turned the faucet on and off. No water came out.

I took a deep breath. "When I asked about your plans, I wasn't criticizing you. I'm talking about right now.

We need to act. The Feux Follets are running amok. There are riots. Basic services no longer work."

He motioned his hand in the air as if waving away the problem.

"Odette was spotted in Illiers." That caught his attention. His gaze cleared and he pursed his lips. "The UNITAS faction has been active," I continued. "Its leaders are heading for New Salem."

He nodded and stared into the distance. A long silence followed. I think he lost track of time.

"An outbreak of La Fièvre Pourpre killed a lot of people at Ambreville Hospital. The outbreak has been contained. According to rumors, someone tried to weaponize the fever."

He managed a crooked smile. "Burnette did that a long time ago. It sounds like someone else has succeeded."

"If you call that success," I said. "The FIOE is striking. The Miners are protesting in sympathy. They are betraying you."

"I know." He tapped the empty water glass on the floor with his fingernail. "I will make plans for them later."

"Amber is no longer being shipped. Trade has come to a halt."

"I see."

"Corruption is rampant. Quartermaster Faraday is robbing the government blind."

"Unimportant." He closed his eyes. Even in this dim room, the quality of Nouveau Haitiah's light seemed to bother the Doctor. Sometimes he complained about it. He said the light was too intense, a kind of neon ultraviolet. "If only I could be a small blue metallic beetle crawling into a crack in the ground."

"People are starving!" I sighed in exasperation. "Are you listening?"

"I hear you."

"You should make a will." I thought that would shake him up. He really did look terrible, lying naked in that bathtub. Not only was he overweight, but he had not been taking care of his skin.

He shrugged. "I want to be cremated." He idly turned the squeaky ceramic spigot. On. Off. On. Off. No water. All at once he cried out: "Victoria! Save me!"

"Save yourself," I fired back.

"How can I? I have been cursed! I have been betrayed!" he wailed.

"Hah! No one betrayed you, no one who matters, and you know it. You betrayed yourself. And what do you mean, 'cursed'?"

"Once, a soldier cursed me. He said 'may you know thirst the rest of your days'."

I crossed my arms and waited. His eyes darted about the room like a cornered animal. "The mind dreams after the body dies."

"Then you better not get cremated."

"Maybe I will perform triage from beyond the grave," he sneered. "Don't write me off just yet."

"Oh please," I said, "spare me. Drama is *my* specialty." I tossed my head and brushed my hair back from each shoulder. No one was better than playing this little game than me. I was *not* going to indulge him, and at that moment I think he realized it.

He changed his tactics and adopted a pleading tone. "Victoria, I still believe. I exist. You exist. Nouveau Haitiah exists. If memory has any meaning at all, if art matters, then it must exist!

"What are you talking about? What must exist?"

"The Fountain of Youth."

I put my hands on my hips. "That's just a story!"

"Not so! Why do you think the Children's Fund fighters look so young? It has something to do with the town of Last Call! Odette knows!"

"Odette? She's a sociopath! And the people at Last Call were poisoned!"

He crossed his arms and looked away.

"What am I going to do with you?" I asked. "Do you really think you can find immortality? Go back to your books, you foolish man. Once you said you wanted to make this world a better place, and silly me, I wanted to help you do it. After the summit at Colombe Habitation you had everything you needed to make it happen. Now look at you! Sitting naked in a bathtub without any water in it! You should have spent your time listening to something real."

"Like what?"

"Your heart."

He snorted. "Now who is being foolish?"

"That's enough. I'm leaving. And put some clothes on!" I turned my back on him and strode towards the bathroom door, my heels clicking purposefully upon the blue tile. I slammed the door, and on the way out, I heard the crash of a glass breaking on the wall behind me. The nerve! He had thrown the empty glass after me! Now shattered shards would litter the tile. The only time I could remember him throwing something like that was in a story he told me about a funeral urn, a long time ago.

I marched down the hall. I was ready to give up on him and walk out of Government House and never come back. I could always go back to Colombe Habitation. Ambreville was too hot and humid anyway, and it was always nice and cool at Colombe Habitation. I was really, really mad, and so help me, I was ready to do it. And then it came to me in a flash of inspiration!

I saw the way.

Returning to the bathroom door, I cracked it open, leaned in, and said in my coyest, most coaxing voice: "Oh, Leon, I was just wondering... If you're not doing anything tomorrow, let's get together and have a little séance! Let's set a trap for Odette."

THE SEANCE

"Victoria, come in."

I crossed the polished floor of the executive parlor with my shoulders thrown back as usual, posture erect, exuding confidence with every step, made real by the solid clack of my favorite navy blue high heels reverberating from the bare wooden walls. I wore a soft light blue dress with a darker blue lace shawl on my shoulders, and a coral pink belt cinched about the waist, giving it just the right accent. For earrings, I wore a pair of dangling black diamonds. The Doctor sat at the large table in the center of the room, facing me and wearing a simple white short-sleeved shirt, black slacks, and brown loafers, which really did not match. Remy stood by his side, wearing his aide-de-camp's uniform, a shiny green three-piece affair that did not flatter his heavy physique. Remy carefully removed an empty water glass, swept up his octagonal amber dice from the desk, and hurried past me, muttering something about finishing the game another time.

I carried a large glass globe- my crystal ball- which I place on the table in the middle of the room. I then went to each corner of the room and lit a diamond root scented candle. In one corner there was a narrow shelf with his personal shrine: a small globe, a miniature mirror, and a tiny pair of amber dice. I knew he did not take them seriously. He once said the small globe represented circular reasoning, that everything was fixed because the dice were loaded, and a lot of other cynical stuff. As far as I could tell, his cynicism was a recent development. I did not notice it until after the summit at Colombe Habitation, where we won our great political victory and went on to eventual political dominance. After taking power, we set up residence here in Government House, in Ambreville. His attempts to save the people of Nouveau Haitiah from poverty and the unending round of violence seemed to result in compromises and ineffective half-measures. On a more personal basis, he voiced complaints about the effects of aging, mostly minor aches and pains, and of course he could not save himself from that either. He also suffered from depression. Falling into cynicism was not a difficult thing to do, I suppose. That was part of the reason for this séance: to help him recapture his focus and commitment to doing something worthwhile; and of course, we both wanted to set a trap for Odette. I was in a pretty good mood until I saw the other corner of his office. The infamous hat rack stood there with its two skulls mounted atop it.

"Who do those belong to?" I asked. I already knew the answer, but I was ready to start something.

"Waterman and Ampere," he shrugged and then laughed. "At least, they used to belong to them."

"You need to get rid of those things," I said. I caught a glint of metallic blue in the orbital socket of Waterman's skull. It was a beetle. "They're disgusting."

"My followers expect me to project a certain image," he said reasonably.

"What image is that? What is wrong with you?"

"Nothing! Since when did you become so sensitive? Don't be naïve."

"I'm not naïve!" I shouted. I was ready to throw something. Instead, I stormed around the room, pulling the shades and closing the bay windows. I wanted to argue, but before I finished, we had a surprise: a disoriented mock mynah flew through the last open window and into the parlor. It was the strangest thing, to see this gaudy red and yellow creature flap and blunder about the room, screeching and squawking "Victoria" as it careened into walls and furniture. I was afraid it would knock over a candle and burn down Government House.

Vic-toooooor-iaaa

After a few minutes of chaos and laughter, I managed to corner it and hold the trembling creature- very carefully- with both hands. I could feel the pounding of its heart. The poor thing was terrified. Taking care it did not scratch or bite, I brought it to the open window and released it back into the wild, then closed the window and drew the drapes.

We sat down at the table and composed ourselves. I pretended to forget about the argument I was ready to start earlier. This was more important. "Are you ready?" I asked. "Is it time for a séance?"

"*Oui*," The Doctor replied.

"You are ready to enter a trance with me?" He re-affirmed his intention. I gave him a half-smile. "You know it's all just psychological projection and intuition, right?"

He nodded. "That can be useful too."

The anise and charcoal odor from the diamond root candles permeated the room. I pulled my chair close to him and took his hands in mine. His hands were slender, his fingers long, and they were still one of his better features, despite his being well into middle age. Reading all those books must have preserved them.

"Look into the sphere. Look into its depths. Look! See the intersection of width and breadth at the crossroads, and the intersection of height and depth, from the center of Nouveau to the sun's center..." I rapidly rapped the table with my knuckles.

The smoke from the diamond root candle filled the room with an intoxicating purple haze. He inhaled deeply and shuddered. "I... this... this thing actually works!"

"Peer inside this crystal ball, this globe, this world, this pearl beyond comparison," I said softly.

"I see," he murmured.

"Tell me what you see."

A scene appeared within the globe of a tall, handsome, charismatic man standing in a sparkling field of purple diamond root. It felt-three dimensional and completely real, including sounds and smells, as if the act of viewing submersed us inside a world within the globe. The man's hands moved with slow compelling grace as he spoke in a deep, mellifluous baritone: "For me, Nouveau Haitiah is quite real."

I pulled myself out of the world within the globe and back to the séance table. "It's Alihak!" I said. "Isn't he handsome? He appears every time. What a powerful man!"

"How often do you do this?" The Doctor asked in wonder.

"Never mind. Keep holding my hand, and concentrate. Let's practice some more before we set the trap. Tell me what else you see." I rapped the table again.

He calmly described his vision to me: "I see you, Victoria. You sit in front of a large ornate mirror, combing your long hair. You are old, very old, but your hair is thick and still black as night. The window next to you lights your face, which is deeply lined with wrinkles. Your hands are spotted and frail. One rests lightly on the table, shaking ever so slightly. With the other you pull a brush through your hair, stroke after stroke. You dwell alone in this tiny one-room apartment, utterly forgotten by the world outside, pining for a love you never even knew you needed; but no one survives in isolation. So how do you, an intelligent creature, spend your dying moment? You spend it the way most denizens of Nouveau Haitiah spend their lives: vain, self-absorbed, and ignored by the world outside your window."

"Oh!" I exclaimed in dismay. I tried to pull my hands away and break the bond, but he held on. I concentrated on my breathing and regained my composure. "Sometimes this can be upsetting," I told him. My voice was a little shaky.

"I want to do it again," The Doctor said eagerly. He gave my hand a squeeze.

"Easy for you to say. I just saw myself right before my death." My experience did not diminish his enthusiasm. From the rapt expression on his face I could see he meant it; he really wanted to go back into the crystal ball. I knew he really cared for me, but today, sympathy was not on the agenda. I swallowed hard. "All right, one more time."

We fell in together, sharing perceptions from somewhere inside this ball in front of me, this globe, this world within a world, this pearl.

This time I described my vision to The Doctor: "Surrounded by darkness, a powerful sense of peacefulness envelops you, and a complete comfort with dependence upon loved ones swells with the last beats of your pounding heart. In your mind, you rise and straighten, and with that act of ascension, you made your last stand. Now, at last, you know how an intelligent being behaves in its dying moment. Charged with a sense of well-being and belonging, you say farewell, and walk into the center of blue-white shimmering light."

He tried to yank his hand away, but I was ready for it, and held tight. Turnaround is fair play! Served him right! That was my little payback for his showing me brushing my hair in my old age. Although I must say, it did not seem fair- the vision of his final moments appeared far more fulfilling and evoked far less pathos than mine; nevertheless, I persevered. As long as we held hands and maintained the trance, we both exerted some control over what we perceived inside the ball. It took a lot of personal power. It required a strong will. He possessed it and so did I. However, we were only spectators of the world inside the crystal ball; neither of us possessed enough power to interact with what we perceived. It was a one-way vision *unless* we encountered another exceptionally powerful person capable of breaking through the veil.

I was counting on it.

"Again?" I asked. He nodded. We concentrated upon the ball.

An old book with creamy pages appeared within the ball, but instead of words and sentences, it lay open to a three-dimensional scene from the Nouveau Haitian jungle, a pond encircled by a narrow beach of black sand. A man floated face down in the dust covered pool, fixed eyes staring at the black and yellow bands of sand below. A puff of wind rippled the water and swayed the tendrils of his long brown hair. Wavelets lapped against his pale skin and sodden safari clothes, casting rows of marching shadows across the pool's floor. From a small vent in the sandy floor, pearl-white bubbles seeped towards the surface, occasionally flowing around his head and chest like effervescent memories.

We both pulled out of the world of the globe at the same time.

"That's me," The Doctor said aloud, shaking his head in wonder. "Is that the Fountain of Youth?"

"That is just a story," I replied impatiently.

"Then what was it?" The Doctor asked.

"I don't know," I admitted, and I wondered: *Did The Doctor die twice? Or not at all?* The pool looked remarkable, and it disturbed me a great deal, but I did not want to let us go astray following every strange will-o-the-wisp that appeared in the crystal ball.

"Put it aside for now," I continued. "Something like that will not matter if Odette catches us unprepared. We need to focus on why we are here. Focus on the barefoot witch. Let her know we are here, in Government House."

A crystal ball, a globe, a world within a world, a pearl beyond compare...

And from the darkness of the ball, Odette spoke:

"It's about time you and I had a talk, don't you think?"

ODETTE

THE UNOFFICIAL HOSTESS

It happened years ago. I remember it very clearly. At the same time the so-called 'Doctor' arrived at the camp near Bois Caiman and infected the world with his presence, I waited in the jungle, not far from the camp of my enemies, the LAR. It was a typical afternoon, hot and humid with a purplish-gray overcast, and I shifted and settled into the crook of a mapou tree above the jungle floor. I watched the sandy path below me, waiting amid the black and violet brown foliage for the signal to spring the ambush. As I bided my time, I was thankful for the mapou's dense foliage; it protected my fair skin from the intense sun at the same time it concealed me from my enemies. The foliage was as dense as the leaves of a book, although leaves of a book were certainly no concern of mine; I know how to read, but I generally choose not to. I prefer the spoken word and oral tradition, because what *I* do is remember. Everything. It's all about memory. So while one hand touched the smooth papery bark, the other rested on the hilt of my black diamond machete, and as I settled into the crook of that tree, I recalled the village where I grew up. I heard their voices:

Save me

Help, I'm burning up

Is there no hope? No antidote?

The voices were female. They sounded like my own voice, but the voices of these deceitful ghosts were real. They were real because my memory made them real. Memory immortalizes the voices of the dead; of course, what they actually say may or may not be true. That is why I call them 'deceitful ghosts': while they may be immortal, they cannot be trusted. That is part of the problem with being a witch: it is hard to tell what is real, what is supernatural, what is imagined… and what happens when all three are one and the same.

Senses can be just as untrustworthy. Funny thing about the senses: I could close my eyes and I would be unable to see; I could close my mouth and be unable to taste; I could hold my breath and be unable to smell; I could withdraw, and avoid touching; but I could not escape the orchestrated sounds of words.

Meanwhile, I dangled my bare feet, and wondered if my enemies would hear the voices when they passed beneath the mapou tree.

Those voices came to me from my childhood memories of the town of Last Call, near the headwaters of the Bimi. Last Call provided Nouveau Haitiah with black diamonds and amber. Its townspeople looked like me: petite, yet athletic, and fair skinned, with reddish- brown or ginger hair. Most had fine features like mine, and hazel eyes.

Many of them died. They were poisoned. According to rumors, someone poisoned the water supply. As a malfacteur, I always made it my business to know about poisons, so a few accused me. But I did not do it. It was the poison of the yew, and there is no antidote for that. So, the survivors abandoned Last

Call. They formed a fighting faction called 'The Children's Fund.' My father, Commissar Ampere, led them, and I joined too. Later, many others came to our banner, including some old men like Chief Harado, Lieden, Sanger, and others, but we were originally called The Children's Fund for good reason: some of us looked like little children, eternally youthful. Some attributed that youthfulness to something special about the headwaters of the Bimi. I think that is just a story. The headwaters of the Bimi are so poisonous, they are dark beyond imagining.

In the greatness of my fear, I changed.

Focusing on anything natural quieted the ghosts, so, I counted the lobes the mapou tree's black and violet brown leaves. Each leaf had eight lobes. I crushed one and released the biting odor of camphor. *Give me the courage to take the first step*, I thought, and rolled the leaf between my fingers until it fell apart. I strained to sense the approach of the enemy, the soldiers of the LAR- the Lord's Army of Resistance.

The snap of a branch alerted me and my heart swelled with anticipation. I adjusted my grip on the machete, peered through the leaves and branches, and spotted ghostly figures winding through the hot jungle in single file. Their track would bring them directly beneath my tree. I could not see the other members of my faction, but I knew Chief Harado, Lieden, and Singer were close. They lurked nearby among the thick purple and citron cycads along either side of the trail.

The first soldier passed, carrying their flag: a black diamond on a yellow background. More marched by my tree. A tall, dark-skinned, muscular soldier brought up the rear. I could read his nametag: 'Korpusant.' The signal came at last, an imitation of the hoarse croak of a crapaud bouga, just as he stepped around the mapou's gnarled roots. Now was the time. My next step would be a leap of faith, from the tree limb down to the body of Korpusant below. I stepped into empty air, gripping the blade of my black diamond machete with both hands. I fell upon the soldier and drove the blade directly into the top of his skull.

He collapsed to the sandy ground. I landed, rolled, and then stood over my victim. Blood flowed from his scalp, but not as much as one would expect with a head wound. I reached into my macoute and withdrew a vial of dull violet powder. After sprinkling some over his face, I poured the rest into my palm, and scattered it to the eight winds. I leaned over Korpusant, loudly clapped my hands together, and spoke: "It's about time you and I had a talk, don't you think?"

KORPUSANT

The plumes of dull violet powder expanded in a globular cloud, much like the interior of a nacreous pearl or a crystal ball. Within the plumes, motes sparkled in the vast interior, like synapses inside a skull's spherical space.

"Am I dead?"

"No, Korpusant." Not yet, I thought; but he did not need to know.

"What happened? The last I remember, I was walking through the jungle on patrol, and something struck me on the top of the head, and everything went black."

"That is exactly what happened."

"So this is magic," he said, more to himself than me. It had more to do with the powder than magic, but I saw no reason to disabuse him of the notion. *"Where am I?"*

I laughed. *"Good question! You are in a world within a world, several times over."*

"Am I dreaming?"

"No. Listen carefully. Have you ever seen those wooden dolls of decreasing size placed one inside the other?"

"No."

I sighed. I should have known better than to use that example. *"All right, never mind. Listen. You are surrounded by my powder and under my control while it lasts. The powder has created a world inside a world- so your world is a world inside my own. I am your Unofficial Hostess."*

"I do not understand. I remember dreaming."

"Yes?"

"I dreamed..."

"What did you dream, Korpusant?"

"I dreamed about a Fountain of Youth."

"Perfect!" I smirked. *"Make sure you mention that to The Doctor when you see him."*

"Who are you?"

"Je m'appelle Odette."

"You're not Victoria."

I laughed. *"The Official Hostess? Obviously not! No, I am not like her. She thinks book knowledge can be a substitute for the knowledge that comes from oral traditions, as if putting something in writing makes it more official! Oh, how she loves her title. Well, I know a better way. Hear me well! I use unofficial channels."*

"I do not understand you at all."

"That is because you are like most people. You forget. You should listen carefully. I do not forget. I remember everything. If you were in my position, you would do the same as me, and listen; if you remembered everything, you would realize it is all a betrayal of one kind of another, whether it is the betrayal of my father, or nature's betrayal of the people of Last Call- and you know what? Betrayal poisons everything. Remember that. Betrayal poisons everything. If you just remember that, then you will do as I do, and deal out your own poisons and powders and deadly perfumes with abandon. Stop pretending

to be a soldier, as if there were some cause to be true to! Just go out and take your revenge!

"You're crazy," Korpusant said.

I laughed. *"And you're not? I have to go. This dusty globe is dispersing, and I have unfinished business outside it. Your comrades will come for you soon."*

I clapped my hands.

TO AMBREVILLE FOR MY REVENGE

Dispensing with memories from years earlier, I focused on what I must do today. I adjusted my macoute, and step by step, made my solitary way towards Ambreville and Government House, each step as inevitable as spoken words entering the porches of an ear, as inevitable as the terrible vengeance I would take upon 'The Doctor' and the Official Hostess, Victoria. I would find them at Government House. Nothing would stop me. Wiping the sweat from my brow, I concentrated on putting one bare foot in front of the other. The trail's packed clay felt good upon the soles of my feet.

Help me.

Ah, the voices of deceitful ghosts.

I dreamed of a Fountain of Youth.

That was Korpusant. His voice was no longer so deep.

"I never killed anyone who didn't deserve it," I declared aloud. I needed a distraction, so I sang in

long suspended tones. The ghosts joined me with
eerie, ethereal harmonies. I marked time with the
slap of my bare feet against the gritty ground. I also
kept the rhythm by shaking my yellow and orange
gourd rattles, one in each hand. My words slurred as I
sang:

Only Leon

Only Leon

Leon only

Leon only

Lonely, lonely

Lonely, lone Lee-oooooon

Solo

So low

So loooong

Each step brought me closer to Ambreville. Each step
aged me an additional second, a minute, mile by mile.
Each left me more experienced, even if the experience
consisted of nothing more than slowly propelling

myself along an unremarkable path through a monotonous savannah of rancid yellow xanthia grass. The closer I came to civilization, the more I controlled my own fate, as well as that of others. Ultimately the same fate awaited all of us: my father was dead; the old men- Chief Harado and Lieden and Singer- were dead. Most of the original members of the Children's Fund had been identified by their youthful appearance and slaughtered by the Feux Follets. Now the Fund was no more. For The Doctor and Victoria I brought the same beginning, middle, and end they brought to me, with all the inevitability of each fall of my small foot. I was fate's harbinger.

Help me.

"No." I said a little too loudly. My passage flushed a mock mynah from the brush. The scarlet creature bolted into the sky and circled above me, singing:

Vic-toooooor-ia

Nature itself mocked me with her name. That would not stand! Victoria would come to know the greatness of her own fear! The deceitful ghosts sensed my anger and became agitated again. One shouted over the others:

I will give you black diamonds. Help me.

"No." Deceitful ghosts would offer me anything if it made me pay attention to them, much like ordinary people. Everyone wanted someone to listen to their story. This ghost from Last Call shrieked and gibbered and punctuated its manifestation with a prolonged wail. I reached into my pale blue macoute and withdrew a vial. The wailing grew louder. I opened the vial and pinched a generous amount of white powder, then gave it a careless flick into the air. The wailing abruptly stopped. "Consigned to oblivion," I said, and laughed in my high girlish voice. Like most ordinary people, the ghost deserved it.

In the greatness of my fear, I changed.

"I know, father." If only he were still alive! It enraged me to hear him reduced to this state. I would avenge him. I would retrieve his skull, pulverize it, and lay it to rest with a proper memento mori outside Ambreville. Right now, his skull decorated a hat rack in Government House. For that, The Doctor would pay!

ON THE OFFENSE

I donned my broad-brimmed hat and saffron veil outside the city limits, put on lemon hued gloves, and changed into a canary yellow dress. When I crossed the river Bimi and entered Ambreville, the Bimi was not some sort of mythical river of forgetfulness, but just the opposite, because I *remember*. Not only would I free my father and the other ghosts, I would liberate the suffering neighborhoods of Ambreville from their own oppressive past, whether they wanted it or not. I brought change! Soon, I passed the 'Lest We Forget' cenotaph at the central crossroads of Ambreville, in the Plaza de l'Exposition Coloniale. The cenotaph appealed to me, because I would never forget my father.

An attractive woman in a red-checked dress was walking on the boardwalk in the opposite direction from me. When she side-stepped a beggar, she momentarily stood in my way. I intentionally gave her a hard shoulder as I passed. No one would stand between me and Government House.

In the greatness of my fear…

"I know, father." Did the shoppers hear the ghost? After all, hearing was a sense which could not be stopped. Sounds and words poured into the ears regardless of a hearer's wishes, so the reality of the spoken word was very powerful, far more powerful than the written one, which could be stopped simply by shutting the eyes. Ah, none of the shoppers reacted to the voice of the ghost. They must not have heard him. *Bon.*

A metallic red arachnofly buzzed past. It seemed like there were more of them in Ambreville of late. The air was thick with airborne arachnids. The city palisades kept out most of the plant and animal life, but not the arachnids. They hurled throw-webs, clicked warnings and come-ons to each other, they looped and barrel rolled and careened off the sides of buildings; all in an endless search to eat and be eaten, to parasitize and produce and reproduce. They were pests, and one more good reason to wear a hat and veil.

The Nouveau Haitian ecosystem did not seem to do well within city limits, but then, neither did the human one. The poor and crippled and cancer ridden swarmed the walkways and stumbled past the stalls of various vendors like so many arachnoflies, all making desperate efforts to barter or steal. I clutched my macoute to my side to discourage pickpockets. The buildings were like the people: simple and ramshackle. Most were wooden one-story affairs selling red and pink beans, limes and candied ginger, as well as gourds and potable water and thin colorful cloth. The cloth was especially popular because there had been a recent Fièvre Pourpre outbreak in the outlying areas and it served nicely as a veil. I adjusted my own and gave myself an occasional spritz of vanilla perfume.

Government House was across the way. I crossed the street, doing my best to keep my bare feet out of the disgusting muck, and climbed the stairs to the porch. A young guard slouched by the side of the doorway, obviously bored. He wore the black pajamas which identified him as a Feux Follet, a fanatical follower of The Doctor. He perked up when I approached.

"Can I help you?" he asked.

"*Oui.*" I pulled my veil aside, tilted my head, and smiled while looking up at him. He shifted his weight from foot to foot, smiling in return. '*Yellow powder or mist?*' I asked myself. I pursed my lips and held up one finger to my lips, and then from my macoute, I pulled a tiny vial. The guard looked puzzled, but before he could react, I pulled the stopper and threw its contents into his face. The clear liquid turned to mist even as it contacted his nose and mouth. I quickly dropped my veil again to avoid inhaling it, and stepped back. The guard fell heavily at my feet. He was dead before he hit the ground.

I opened the door without knocking and a clumsy arachnofly exited over my head and buzzed towards the cenotaph. I entered. A large desk occupied the reception area, with a portly man in a three-piece green suit sitting behind it, idly rolling amber dice on the wooden table. I lifted my veil.

"*Bonjour*, Remy. It's about time you and I had a talk, don't you think?"

PRESSING THE ATTACK

"Odette! What are you doing here?" Remy started to rise from his seat.

I closed the door behind me and raised one gloved hand. "Stay seated, Remy." My other hand slipped into my macoute.

He remained in his chair, eyes wide, and raised both hands in a gesture of surrender. His lower lip trembled. "Please, Odette. Don't kill me. I'm unarmed. I've never done anything to hurt you."

"My business today is not with you. Where are Victoria and The Doctor?"

"Upstairs." His mouth gaped and he shook his head in disbelief. "How did you get past the guard?"

"I smiled." Out of the corner of my eye I spotted a hat rack with two skulls on it. I padded across the hardwood floor with my bare calloused feet. The surface felt smooth and cool. "This is mine." I stood on my tiptoes, lifted my father's skull, and tenderly placed it in my bag.

In the greatness of my fear, I changed.

"Hush," I said.

Remy looked confused. "The Doctor will be unhappy if you take that. It's his favorite decoration."

"He'll be a lot unhappier when he sees me. Stay where you are, Remy. Don't move."

As I turned to exit the room for the stairs, Remy apparently found his courage. "Don't do it, Odette. Feux Follets are guarding them. They will kill you on the spot, no questions asked."

I gave a crooked smile. "I am not afraid of the Feux Follets. Tell you what. Call Victoria and The Doctor. Have them come downstairs."

Remy shook his head. "The Doctor is sick in bed. Victoria is tending to him."

"Then I will go to them." I pulled down my veil, strode into the main landing, and faced a steep flight of stairs, gloved hand already in my macoute.

A Feux Follet with a broad chest and enormous neck-
perhaps the strongest man I have ever seen- was
rapidly descending the steps and already near the
bottom. He was almost upon me before I could react.
The Feux Follet reached for my free arm. I stepped
back to elude his grasp, and threw a handful of yellow
powder into his face. His eyes widened as his
momentum carried him past me. He collapsed on the
floor in a heap and did not move again. I pulled his
machete from its scabbard, and used my other hand
to grab an additional handful of yellow powder.

Remy was calling out a warning from the reception
room behind me. His cries would alert the entire
building. If he dared remain in Government House
when I finished upstairs, I would make him pay for
that. I strode towards the stairway, confident my
poisons and razor sharp knife would suffice.

Two more Feux Follets came down the stairs, one well
ahead of the other. These two were better prepared.
Both carried black diamond machetes in their hands.
As I approached the stairs, I changed speeds, and
threw myself into the first Feux Follet as he reached

the bottom. We both swung our knives, and missed; I threw another handful of powder, and he died instantly, temporarily blocking my path up the staircase. The second Feux Follet halted midway down the stairs. He could not reach me, but I was too far away to take him down with powder. I threw my machete. It was a good throw. It hit him in the throat and he dropped his weapon. He sank to his knees, clutching his neck with both hands while his blood spurted upon the stairs and banister.

Holding on to the banister, I stepped past the bodies with care, but the blood was unavoidable. It stained my yellow dress and made the surface slippery. There was no time to wash my bare feet. I had to press the attack. I picked up another machete from one of my victims and climbed the stairs. The veil was still in place, the macoute was at my side, and my gloves were intact, so I was in business if I wanted to use the powder again.

My next opponent stood at the top of the stairs. This Feux Follet was older, with gray hair and a tall, wiry frame. Like the others, he was barefoot and wore the traditional black pajamas, but this one exhibited more caution than the others. He was probably a veteran. He was testing the balance of his machete; he must have seen the way I dispatched my previous enemy, because as he backed away, I could tell he wanted to throw his at me. He retreated a few more steps down the hall. I reached the top and cautiously took a few steps towards him. He backed his way into a door at the end of the hallway. This was a smart opponent. He was much stronger than me and he could physically overwhelm me, but if he allowed me to get close, I would use my powder or mist. If he could stall long enough, reinforcements might arrive. But he could retreat no further. He already knew what I could do with a machete. If I threw first, he would probably die on the spot. Even though I knew it was coming, the Feux Follet still managed to surprise me by attacking first. Instead of winding up for a throw, he whipped his knife underhand with a flick of the wrist. A black diamond machete is extraordinarily sharp; it does not need to be thrown hard to cause great harm. Fortunately for me, it was a bad throw, low and to one side. I hurled myself away from it, but the machete still severed my Achilles tendon. For a moment I was too stunned to act. I had been overconfident, and now I was in serious trouble. Pushing off with my good foot, I charged the Feux Follet and swung my machete. It was a bad swing. My feet were slick with blood and I lost my balance. Weaponless, he swatted my swing aside and made me miss by a lot, but in doing so he was left in a poor position. I was on my knees, and he was off balance with his back partially turned to me. I slashed at his arm without much force. The knife sliced off half his bicep. He yelled, panicked, and then fell hard against the door. He turned his back and pounded on the door for someone to open it. No one did. He should have tried the doorknob, but that is what panic will do to a person. I put all of my weight on one foot and took better aim, and swung, and took off the top of his head.

I took a deep breath and tried the doorknob. It turned. If the barefoot veteran had simply gone through the door, he would still be alive, and I would be in a very bad situation. I pushed the door open and scanned the room for traps. It was empty. There was

a door directly opposite from me. I wiped one hand
on my dress and also wiped the machete handle on it,
smearing red blood on the canary yellow fabric. I
adjusted my veil, checked my macoute, and made
sure the strap was secure across my shoulder. The
bag was heavier than usual because of the skull. My
heel was bleeding and I felt a little woozy, but there
was nothing I could do about that now. I would have
to remember to use my good bare foot if I needed
traction for an attack. I reached into my pale blue
macoute, grasped more yellow powder in my palm,
and stepped into the room.

The door on the other side creaked open. Victoria
stood on the threshold, her hands at her side.

"*Bonjour*, Victoria." I took another step. The
hardwood floor felt gritty beneath my calloused feet.
"It's about time you and I had a talk, don't you think?"

"There's no time, malfacteur. Say what you have to
say. Make it quick."

"I'm here for The Doctor. I'm here for you." I swayed
unsteadily. I had never felt so dizzy. Something was
very wrong. It was more than a matter of losing blood

through my heel. Both of my feet felt like they were on fire and the flames were climbing my legs.

"Look down," Victoria said.

I wanted to throw the machete at The Official Hostess, but my hands were numb. The machete dropped from my grasp and bounced on the gritty hardwood. The strap of my macoute slipped from my shoulder and dropped, and my father's skull rolled free of the bag. I lowered my chin, my knees gave, and I collapsed. My head hit the floor, and after blinking several times, my eyes focused on its surface. The floor was covered with a fine, gritty powder. I gasped.

"You have poisoned me."

Save me.

Help, I'm burning up.

Is there no hope? No antidote?

A horrible realization came to me: the voices of those deceitful ghosts had belonged to me all along.

"I did not poison you," Victoria said. "You poisoned yourself when you chose to enter this room in bare feet. That powder could only work when pressed into bare skin."

I fought down the panic rising in my chest. "Are you going to turn me into a zombie?"

She laughed. "Of course not. There is no such thing; besides, malfacteur, I am not that kind of a witch. I am The Official Hostess."

My eyes were failing. I could no longer see. "Save me."

The next voice belonged to the Doctor. "She comes from Last Call. Ask her about the Fountain of Youth. She knows! If she talks, give her the antidote."

"I know, but I will not tell you." The darkness was about to take me. "I curse you, Victoria. In old age, drown in that pool that is your vanity mirror. And you, Doctor… May you know thirst the rest of your days."

I could no longer speak. I could no longer see or even hear. My face was wet with tears. I was afraid of death and I was afraid of the pain. The poison had numbed me at the same time it set my entire body on fire. Gathering myself for one last supreme effort, I turned my head away and, in the greatness of my fear, I smiled.

Leon

THE FOUNTAIN OF YOUTH

I tilted my ceramic canteen high and gloried in the sensation of cold, refreshing water pouring down my throat. After swallowing my fill, I wiped the back of my hand across my mouth with great satisfaction. Replacing the canteen on my belt, I stood with my hands on my hips, shoulders back, and black boots planted firmly on the worn gray wooden planks of the Bimi River pier. Wavelets lapped the huge, mossy, interlocking octagonal stones along the riverbank, and the sun's intense blue-white light reflected off the wavelets, creating a glare. I wiped my sweaty brow and smiled. Everything felt right. Although I was in late middle age, I was in the best shape of my life. I knew where I going and what I was doing, although others might disagree about both means and end. I felt compelled. It was time for me to undertake my own personal migration.

Using one hand to shield my eyes, I inhaled deeply and scanned my surroundings, drinking in the elements. A welcome breath of wind blew back my long brown hair. The air was humid, as usual. Nearby, the Bimi Road sloped down to the river's shore, and disappeared into the waters of the Bimi. The road ran back from the river like a broad ramp into Ambreville, and from there, back to the Way of the Saints, the jungles of Bois Caiman, and sullen hinterlands.

Below me, a portly man worked in a boat, the Santeria. I waited for him to stop. Behind me, the Market Day crowd milled about. Impoverished men and women ran their errands, and unlike the portly man in the boat, they noticed me. One crippled veteran who had been begging for alms called to me in a high, quavering voice: "Leon! Remember me? We fought together at Phosphor Plain!" An old man in the crowd raised his cane high in the air, and a woman waved her amber and black kerchief back and forth like a flag. Another woman raised her baby girl over her head to see me. Next to her stood a wan, whip thin young man who attended University with me many years ago. I recognized another in the crowd, an attractive woman in a red-checked dress. She wore a bracelet of blue beads on her narrow wrist, the same one I remembered. She made a ritualistic gesture, blessing me with the sign of the crossroads. The University student yawped in surprise as twin boys jostled past. They shouted and pushed towards the front of the crowd to get a better look at me. Their parents were nowhere in sight, so the twins might have been orphans- it was not uncommon. They were dressed in rags and their skin was dark from playing in the sun. Both boys were thin and wiry, with short dark hair and dark eyes. It would not have surprised me if they made their living by stealing and picking pockets. One clasped a blue-white toy ball. It was probably his only possession.

"Get your lectra ray, grilled and hot and oh so juicy!" The cries of the vendor hawking lectra ray filled the air. Eating lectra ray struck me as odd. Everyone said Nouveau Haitian flora and fauna were incompatible with human digestive systems. The indigenous life could not gain sustenance from humans, and vice versa. Yet the firm white meat of lectra ray fins, seared over an open fire and sprinkled with minced ginger, were now routinely devoured with pleasure, and seemed to provide nutrition.

Another portion of the crowd gathered on the riverbank around a dead white whip. It was a small one, to be sure; nevertheless, it caused a stir. The finder of the limp carcass offered it to the highest bidder, although whether anyone would bother to bid remained open to question; a dead white whip was a curiosity, to be sure, but inedible and of no possible use, other than being a cause for alarm. It certainly alarmed me, given my experience years ago, when one electrocuted me near this very place. The migration was not supposed to be due for another year, but if it was starting early, then white whips might pose a serious threat to anyone on the river. These football shaped creatures used their long tails as a means of propulsion and to shock prey. They deserved their fearsome reputation, but reputation could not spare this dead one from being the object of derision and entertainment for the boisterous twin boys, who dared one another to poke it.

I wanted to help these twin boys. I wanted to help everyone here in the Market Day crowd, but so far, my efforts to provide peace and stability through responsible government had met with limited success. Victoria enjoyed greater success through her charities, but still, it was not enough. The daily lives of ordinary people remained difficult, and so, I decided on a different tack. The people needed inspiration. They needed a reason to hope. Therefore, I was taking the largest craft on the Bimi, the _Santeria_, upriver in a well-advertised expedition of exploration. Since it was rare to see a working ceramic engine in the first place, that was cause for excitement in itself, but considering I was bound for the headwaters of the Bimi, it was natural for everyone to assume I sought to re-open the black diamond mines in Last Call; if that succeeded, it would prove a huge economic boon for the working people of Ambreville.

Of course, that was not the real mission. I sought the Fountain of Youth.

Now, that was not the kind of thing one could announce to a Market Day crowd. With all the

294

frustration and resentment bubbling beneath the surface, a riot was an ever-present possibility, despite the dampening presence of the Ambreville Police. The crowd might forget its fear of the Police, turn into a mob, and rush the Santeria, demanding to be taken along; or, they might attack the crew because the trip was an obvious waste of time. Another reason not to announce the real goal was the outside possibility someone would organize a competing expedition.

I made assumptions. I assumed that a Fountain existed, and that it could be found at the headwaters of the Bimi. Before she died, I asked Odette if she knew about the Fountain, and she said, "I know." I assumed she was telling the truth, especially since she refused to provide any details about it, not even for the antidote that would save her from an agonizing death. In addition, the flag of the Children's Fund had a stylized fountain on its field, as did Odette's macoute. Korpusant dreamed about a Fountain after I brought him back. And during the séance, I saw a vision of a pool with a man floating in it, face down; that could have been the Fountain. It made sense. I had come to Nouveau Haitiah for a reason. I came to save people and to save myself, or as Alihak once put it, to redeem time and memory. I came to find a cure for old age and disease and death, and incredibly, it was possible. It could be done! The solution was within my reach, and the Fountain would provide the way to do it. I saw the way.

Meanwhile, the short, stocky man aboard the Santeria remained oblivious to me as he continued working. The portly orderly and aide-de-camp, Remy, wore the heavy baffled clothes of a laborer, and they were already soaked with perspiration. Absorbed in his task, he arranged the heavy crates on the crowded wooden deck. I hailed him.

"Well, it's about time! Come aboard, give me a hand. I'm drenched!"

"Is it the heat?" I asked.

"It's not the heat, it's the humidity."

We both laughed at the old punch line, and I boarded the Santeria. We hugged and slapped each other's back. I pointed out the cause of Remy's copious sweating. "Look," I said, "you are overdressed. It is hotter and more humid here by the river. Wear what I am wearing." I wore safari style attire, with a light shirt and khaki trousers.

Remy shook his head. "I can't afford it." I knew for a fact that he could afford it. The benefits of governing included easy access to public and private money- other people's money, but access nonetheless- and unlike Quartermaster Faraday, Remy never hesitated help himself; nevertheless, I let the matter of attire slide.

Remy ducked into the pilothouse and called back to me. "How can I know what to wear if I don't know where we are going?"

"Upriver," I answered. "It will be hot. Here, take this." I handed him the only book any of us brought along, my copy of *Redeeming Time and Memory* by Alihak. "Put this in the pilothouse where it will not get wet."

Remy complied and returned for another crate. "So we are going up the Bimi. Then what?"

Some bystanders were close enough to hear us, so I did not reply. Remy poked his head out of the pilothouse. He saw me scanning the crowd. "Do you see any of your friends?" The way Remy said 'friends' made no secret of how he really felt about them. Remy crossed the deck, opened the hatch, and descended into the shallow hold.

"They are coming," I replied. "Fernal should be here any moment."

"He's a Feux Follet," Remy declared in a flat tone. Remy had crossed paths with Fernal many times. Although both Remy and Fernal had once belonged to the Lord's Army of Resistance, the same organization that spawned the Feux Follets cult, Remy never participated in religious fanaticism. Like most Nouveau Haitians, he was superstitious, but only insofar as omens, portents, signs, and other forms of magical foreshadowing applied directly to him; otherwise, he did not care. He was a practical man, and a loyal man, but not a particularly brave one. He did not have the stomach for zealotry, secret police, torture, and such. Perhaps his own portliness made him more sensitive.

Remy faced me from the hatchway at the aft. He ran his thick stubby fingers across his round chin. "I've never seen a working outboard motor before. That sure is something. It really draws a crowd!"

I passed a heavy crate down to him. "Careful. Grenades."

He took it from me and carried the crate into Santeria's hold. "An engine... a lot of spare parts... explosives... we must be rolling the dice for high stakes," he called from below. When I failed to respond, he stopped fishing. He climbed out of the hold, faced me, and in a low voice, said what he really thought: "Look, I know the goal of this mission is supposed to be a secret. I understand why you would bring a Feux Follet. He will be loyal to you. That matters. But I do not understand why you chose the others."

"To go upriver, we need the Santeria. The fact we are using the Santeria draws attention. I may be in command, but we still have to deal with political factions, and we need their support. Franklin represents the interests of the black diamond industry-"

"-You mean the Stoners?"

"The Miners," I corrected him with a smile. Franklin would probably bring along a lot of diamond root. "And Galvani represents the interests of the amber trade and what used to be the Joule Syndicate. They both have strong backgrounds in mineralogy, and we will be heading towards a region critically important for the black diamond and amber industries."

"They're both spies."

"I'm counting on it."

"Anyway, it's not them that worry me. Women don't belong on the river."

"Neither do men," I pointed out.

"That's not what I meant," Remy said. "The redhead-"

"-Koppes is a scientist-"

"-is a witch."

"-is a highly respected naturalist," I continued, "specializing in the tropical flora of the NH interior. She represents the interests of the University."

Remy rolled his eyes. "The University has not existed for years. I can't think of anything more useless than a student, unless it's a student blundering around in the jungle."

I used to study at the University, and I happened to take one of her classes, but I let that one pass. "Fair enough, Remy. Call the survivors of the University 'the academic community' or whatever you want. It still exists, you know. They do not care about politics, and her knowledge will come in handy in the jungle. This is a once-in-a-lifetime research opportunity for her. We are going into unexplored territory; little is known about the jungle beyond the banks of the Bimi." I could not resist goading him. "Of course, now that you mention it, Koppes does have long red hair, kind of like a..."

"She's a witch, just like Victoria."

I laughed. "Not every woman who is smarter than you is a witch."

He started to say something, but apparently thought better of it. Clearing his throat, Remy bent down to open a crate. "If there is a problem with her, it is her age," he said without looking at me. "She does not have the stamina to go far from the Santeria."

"Neither does Victoria. Neither do you."

"Victoria and I do," Remy said. "We spent years in the field together. Remember?"

"That is true." He was right. I remembered. A flash of silver caught my eye. In mid-channel, a school of flicker fish leapt through the air, and then sliced back into the Bimi. It was as if the river was calling me. I worked with Remy in silence for a few minutes.

"Where is Fernal?" Remy asked. "I thought he would be here by now. The Feux Follets always say '*the soul migrates to water.*' You'd think Fernal would make a beeline for the Santeria."

I paid no attention to him because in the middle of the Bimi, a spout erupted. A large mollymander was surfacing for air, its misty spume sparkling in the sunlight. Its fountain commanded my gaze, and the bass hiss of its exhalation made me feel again as if the river itself was calling. The great arching brown back and dorsal fin had a crisscross pattern of bright pink with violet undertones; the undertones teased my eye, as if promising more, yet always remaining just beyond the scope of my visible perception, an ultraviolet pattern in an alien spectrum. The blue and maroon feather gills on either side of its enormous, shovel-shaped head were visible even from the distance, yet the greater part of its body remained unseen. Arching its back, the creature slipped beneath the surface.

"Here's Fernal," Caleb announced.

The crowd at the marina parted for the tall, dark-skinned, barefoot man. Fernal padded across the gray wooden pier in loose fitting clothes that resembled pajamas; they were subtly patterned with alternating diamond shapes, like the black and amber back of an eight-legged toad, the crapaud bouga. Fernal looked like he was more ready to take a nap than a trip, and yet, despite his somewhat absurd appearance, no one laughed. The Feux Follets believed life was an electrical manifestation, a will-o'-the-wisp. Members of the cult had the reputation of being strange, fanatical, and fierce warriors, with their devotion focused upon me. The crowd parted for Fernal without a word.

I greeted him. The Feux Follet, a handsome dark-skinned man with broad shoulders, narrow hips, an aquiline nose, and fine regular features, responded to my greeting with a ritualistic gesture, the sign of the crossroads. Although Remy and Fernal knew one another from past encounters, including the infamous negotiation on the Phosphor Plain, Remy ignored him today. I thought he muttered something under his breath- it sounded like "creepy bastard"- but I let it go, and welcomed Fernal aboard the Santeria. Remy extended his arms and said "hand me that crate." Fernal pitched in, and we loaded the hold with provisions.

Remy wiped the sweat from his broad brow. "I hope everybody likes red beans and limes, because we sure loaded a lot! How far up the Bimi are we going, anyway?"

I shielded my eyes with my hand and looked upriver across the broad, silted waters. A riot of purple, yellow, and brown vegetation bracketed the channel, giving the only indication of where the river ended, and the banks began. Were the marina onlookers listening? Should I tell Remy the truth? Remy and I went way back. He was the first person I remembered meeting on Nouveau Haitiah, after I crawled on my hands and knees from that dust covered pool; however, as much as I respected him, I was even more devoted to attaining my goal. The Bimi called me. I needed to go upriver. What I wanted was somewhere up there. This was my last, best hope for saving the people of Nouveau Haitiah, including me. This was my chance for finding a cure, and overcoming death itself. The others would refuse to go if they knew my real goal. Where did devotion to truth and friends stand in relation to something as compelling as overcoming death?

So I answered him. I lied.

"We are going to Last Call for black diamonds."

ON THE BIMI

A hard elbow to the ribs woke me. I rolled across
Santeria's wooden deck in the dark, away from the
source of the blow. Rubbing my ribs, I gathered my
wits, and realized the elbow had come from the
scientist, Koppes.

It was hot and humid, so at night we stripped down to
our underwear and slept on the cool, hard deck.
While sleeping, I must have nestled against her. A
sharp elbow was my reward. Shaking my head, I sat
up and gazed at the hazy night sky. Stars glowed in
the soft tropical night, small white points embedded
in darkness. In that starlight I could just make out
Koppes' back and pale, freckled arms. She shifted her
sleeping position on the deck, and I sensed from her
breathing that she might be awake. Victoria slept
near the bow. Remy, Galvani and Franklin slept in the
pilothouse. They spent most of their time there
eating, throwing amber dice, smoking diamond root,
and sleeping it off, to do the same the following day.
We were only a few days from Last Call, and for that I

was thankful. Franklin was a quiet man who generally kept to himself, but his habit of cracking his knuckles was becoming irritating. Galvani was short, noisy, and ill-favored, with black oily hair and an aggressive manner, and he kept pestering Victoria. Up to this point, his leers and sexual innuendos were being ignored. Remy, her aide-de-camp, would protect her, of course- Remy adored her- but Galvani failed to realize it was not Remy he needed to worry about. Clearly he did not know who he was dealing with, and I suspected it would not end well for him. The heat remained incredible, even on the water at night, and it was only a matter of time before tempers flared. We all looked forward to reaching our destination as soon as possible.

During the day I socialized with Victoria and Koppes. The women were both well read and intelligent, but aside from their gender and a love for knowledge, Victoria and Koppes had little in common. Victoria was very feminine, classically beautiful, and possessed a high degree of social intelligence. It was no coincidence that she was the Official Hostess. Although Koppes was attractive in her own athletic way, the Professor cared nothing for clothes or shoes or social causes. She was a rationalist who focused on math, science, and logic.

Fernal was loyal to me, but not much of a conversationalist, so when Victoria and Koppes were unavailable, I read Alihak's great work *Redeeming Time and Memory* to help pass the time. At night I watched the stars, and wondered whether there was such a thing as the music of the spheres. It seemed doubtful, to say the least.

Behind me in the darkness, the Feux Follet sat stiffly upright next to the engine, holding the tiller on a steady course, and guiding the <u>Santeria</u> up the Bimi's deep central channel. The wake was marked by phosphorescence; the churning action of the engine's ceramic propeller stirred up unknown forms of microbial life in the water, creatures too small to be seen- an alien world within an alien world. The craft seemed to sit in the middle of the great river, unmoving, while indistinct banks slipped past. Vast mats of blue-green water canopia made the shoreline even more difficult to discern. Suddenly, Fernal steered the <u>Santeria</u> hard to starboard. Moments later, he corrected course back to port.

"What was it?" I asked.

"Dead tree," he answered.

Thankfully, the starlight was bright enough to see some of the snags and sandbars that bracketed the central channel. I tried to relax and listen to the sounds of the Nouveau Haitian night; not even the regular manmade chugging of the engine nor the water sluicing from the bow could drown out the orchestra of amphibians. They chirped, croaked, and warbled, luring one another into symbiotic relationships. Although it sounded like chaos to me, the naturalist Koppes would probably call it a symphony, at least to the ears of those creatures.

A series of loud cracks, like snapping branches, erupted from the left shore, followed by a long, drawn out, high pitched wail. It suddenly cut off. The amphibian chorus abruptly stopped. A series of bubbling, flutelike noises broke the jungle's silence; the notes accelerated and rose in pitch, ending in a series of explosive chuckles.

"Did you hear that?" I asked.

"A crapaud bouga," Fernal answered in his deep voice.

"A crapaud bouga," Koppes echoed. She had been awake after all.

"It must be very big," I said.

"Very big," Fernal agreed.

"It probably made a kill," Koppes added. "They are intelligent predators, but when it comes to reproduction, they are parasites too, like everything else. Full grown, they are almost as big as you, Fernal; strong, too. Its plated jaws can crush this gunwale." She patted the side of the <u>Santeria</u> for emphasis.

"Does it give the kill to its mate?" Fernal asked. I looked at the seated Feux Follet and caught him gazing at me steadily, as if accusing me of something. Up until now, I had accepted his loyalty without question based on his being a member of the Feux Follets. How much did he remember about my time as a 'doctor' for the LAR at Bois Caiman? Did he blame me for failing to save Korpusant?

Victoria came over to join us and answered Fernal's question. "No. There is no mating. There are no mates."

"She's right," Koppes said. "There are no differentiated sexes." That statement was obvious to me and Victoria, but it would probably be lost on Fernal, who had no formal education; of course, that would not stop the scientist from pontificating. "They resemble viruses more than animals. Since there is no differentiation, there is no mating, and therefore no territoriality. They manifest possessiveness when competing for resources such as food, water, access to minerals, and so on, but generally speaking, they make no territorial claims. There is competition within species for hosts, but reproduction does not depend on any kind of societal bonding. Nouveau Haitian flora and fauna act as individuals. They may live and move in groups as they seek the same resources, and they may enjoy one another's company, but they are genetically almost identical, so they always pursue their own individual interests."

"Like us," Fernal joked.

"I don't know about that," Koppes said.

"Everything eats each other," I said, "and at the same time, the flora and fauna need each other to reproduce. It is as if the entire planet were really just one organism."

"It's a good thing they usually leave us alone," Victoria said. "If they didn't, we wouldn't stand a chance." We lapsed into silenced as the jungle cacophony resumed, slowly and tentatively at first, and soon just as loudly as before.

I sat on the bench next to the gunwale, closed my eyes, and listened to the water slide beneath the hull. The crew still did not know the real goal of the mission. Should I tell them? How would they react?

A series of splashes near the craft's stern interrupted my thoughts. The splashes followed one another quickly, like a rock skipping across water.

"What was that?" Fernal asked in a low voice from the aft.

"Just a school of flicker fish," Koppes answered.

"No, it's not flicker fish." Fernal pointed at the phosphorescent wake. "Something is following us. There!" Suddenly Fernal stood and indicated a spot close to the <u>Santeria's</u> stern. "See? Under the water! A blue light!"

I grabbed the bench and leaned forward, peering at the area where Fernal was looking.

A tremendous blow struck the stern from beneath the boat, so powerful it lifted the <u>Santeria</u> from the water. The boat lurched upwards and rolled to port, throwing me into the gunwale. Fernal, standing closest to the point of impact, was thrown from the boat. He somersaulted in mid-air and plunged into the Bimi. A fountain of water splashed high in the air, its expanding concentric circles marking where he disappeared below the surface.

The boat rocked wildly. Cries came from Galvani, Franklin, and Remy inside the pilothouse, but only Remy emerged. Another blow directly beneath the pilothouse jolted the boat. Remy fell to his hands and knees, and the cries from inside the pilothouse abruptly stopped.

With no one at the helm and the engine still running, the Santeria turned in a half-circle, now heading for the canopia mats and the jungle shore.

Keeping my grip on the bench, I peered into the darkness at the point where Fernal went under. He broke the surface, spluttering, arms wildly flailing.

Galvanized into action, I shouted "I will save him," and stood, intending to dive overboard.

Koppes grabbed my arm and pulled me back. "No! Don't do it! Look!"

A blue flash from underwater illuminated the churning waters around Fernal. He momentarily froze in a position that looked as if he was climbing a ladder. Before he could sink, a thick white tentacle erupted from the boiling surface, and in the blink of an eye, coiled around Fernal. Another blue flash lit the waters. It came from a single source, a large oval shape just beneath the surface. The creature dove fast, taking Fernal down with it, down into the dark depths of the Bimi's central channel, descending towards the center of Nouveau Haitiah.

Koppes made for the helm, sat down, and grabbed the tiller. I followed and shook her shoulder. "We have to save him."

She roughly pushed me away. "Let go of me! We can't save him. It's no good."

The roar of my heartbeat seemed to pound in my ears. She was right, of course. No one knew better than me what a white whip could do, and this one was enormous. Fernal was beyond help. Meanwhile, the <u>Santeria</u> was listing to port.

"We're sinking!" Remy cried. "I can't swim!" Tears were running down his cheeks and his eyes were round with panic. Victoria tried calming him, but to no avail.

The dark silhouette of vegetation marking the river bank loomed closer. I turned to Remy and Victoria. "Remy! Are we sinking? Are you sure?"

"Yes."

"Then bail!"

Koppes adjusted the throttle. "I'm holding this course," she said tightly. "I'm putting in for the shore."

"Will we make it?" Victoria asked. At least she was holding it together.

"I think so," Koppes said, "but we're taking on water fast."

"Steer us into the bank," I said. "Ground us. Maybe we can fix it."

Losing the <u>Santeria</u> would be a disaster, but now it looked like we would make the riverbank without risking immersion in the Bimi. "Where are Franklin and Galvani?" I asked.

Remy paused from his bailing to wipe the tears from his eyes, and then shook his head. "Something smashed through the floor of the pilothouse. It threw Franklin against the wall. I think he broke his neck. It looks really bad. Galvani was dragged through an opening in the floor."

"Fernal is dead too," I said.

"White whips," Koppes added. "At least two of them."

"Once I encountered a small stray," I said, "and it nearly killed me. I did not know they could get as big as this."

"There are blockers and there are fertilizers," Koppes explained. "The blockers are drones. Their electrical charge is not as powerful. The fertilizers use their shocks to kill threats, and prepare potential hosts for a parasitic colonization of the lungs. The parasites in the lungs take years to fully develop."

"The blue light in the water," Victoria observed.

"Right," Koppes agreed, "and it gets worse. Stray individuals occasionally swim up from the ocean and show up near Ambreville, but they show in force when they migrate. This must be the season. They're migrating up the Bimi.

"The river will be swarming with them," Victoria said.

"Correct. The blockers will form a series of living walls across the Bimi from Ambreville to Last Call. They will only let fertilizers cross."

"We can't get through?" Remy asked. His efforts to bail had slackened considerably as it became apparent we would safely make it to the shore.

"No," Koppes replied. "If we try, we'll be electrocuted and pulled to the bottom, just like Fernal and Galvani."

The Santeria plowed through a thick mat of water canopia as it slid into the bank of the Bimi, under a canopy of trees so low, they brushed the top of the pilothouse. Using ropes, we secured the boat against the bank.

I went into the pilothouse with Koppes. It was knee-deep with water. Franklin's body was crouched in a corner, his neck at an unnatural angle. The onset of panic rose in my chest, and I fought it down. I needed to concentrate on keeping the rest of us alive, so I focused on examining the large hole in the hull. It was easily visible even under a foot of water. Koppes pulled a tarp from a storage locker and prepared a shroud for Franklin.

"Can that hole can be fixed?" I asked her.

She gave me a withering stare. "No."

"I agree. Victoria, Remy, let's spend the night here. First, let's take care of the bodies of our fellow crewmembers. It looks like cremation will not be an option, so we will have to sew them into tarps and bury them in the Bimi. Tomorrow we will load up as many supplies as we can carry and go upriver by land, to Last Call." My copy of *Redeeming Time and Memory* was on a high shelf. With regret I realized I would have to leave it with the <u>Santeria</u>.

"There will only be four of us," Koppes said matter-of-factly.

Victoria covered her face with her hands. "What will we do without Fernal and Franklin and Galvani?"

"We'll be safe," Remy said. "The river is too dangerous."

Koppes shook her head. "The jungle is worse than the river."

KOPPES

Arachnoflies swarmed around our heads, and the bites were painful. The skin on the back of my neck was exposed, and my bulky backpack made swatting them difficult. I reapplied ohm's moss, a natural repellant, but to no avail; the arachnoflies detected the diamond root in my perspiration. I knew I should not have smoked Franklin's diamond root with Remy the night before. Now they tormented both of us, but left Victoria and Koppes alone.

We followed the road- or rather, what used to be a road- to Last Call. Most of it was overgrown by jungle. I adjusted my backpack and led the way, followed by Victoria, Remy, and Koppes. The incessant, irritating chirping of cycad hoppers made conversation difficult, so I worked off my frustration by slashing through the entangling curtains of hose vines. Chopping the vines with my machete released soaking sprays of potable lukewarm water, which gave some relief from the biting flies. Refreshed, we made better time, and left the din of the cycad hoppers behind us.

From time to time a flock of scarlet mock mynahs would burst from the treetops and circle our small group, singing for all they were worth:

Vic-toooooor-iaaa

It was as if they were welcoming her home. She found it amusing, but it drove the rest of us crazy.

We talked about what happened to Fernal, Galvani, and Franklin, but truly, I barely knew them. Anyway, Remy and I were too worn by the exertion of the trek, the relentless heat, and the humidity. We simply did not have the energy to go through the motions of grieving. Remy had packed Franklin's supply of diamond root and smoked a little at every break, claiming it was in Franklin's honor. He talked incessantly about Last Call and acquiring black diamonds and what he would do with all that wealth. I ignored him. By now, my real goal was all I thought about- the Fountain of Youth.

Only Victoria had the decency to pretend she cared about the lives of those men, but she soon lapsed into an introspective silence. Koppes never expressed any feelings one way or another. She did not care about

Korpusant or the Feux Follets religion, nor did she care for gambling, social activities, or mineralogy. The subject of amber interested her, but only from a scientific perspective. She focused on the flora, and I have to admit, her knowledge proved invaluable.

I wiped the sweat from my brow. Overhead, occasional breaks in the canopy revealed a high overcast. The bruised yellow-gray sky signaled the onset of rain. Wind gusts shook the dry cycad fronds, and they rattled like a chorus of percussion instruments. In the distance, thunderclaps rumbled.

"I wish it would rain," I said.

"The heat is horrible," Victoria said.

"No point in complaining," Koppes chirped in a matter of fact tone.

"It's not the heat, it's the humidity," Remy joked.

I rolled my eyes and did not dignify the stale joke with a response, instead forging ahead through the thick purple and dull lilac undergrowth, swinging my machete in wide swathes. Victoria, Remy, and Koppes followed in single file, trudging through muck and shallow puddles. Peals of thunder grew more distinct as the squall approached.

"How far do you think it is to the black diamonds?" Remy asked.

"Are we there yet?" Victoria teased.

With my next step I sank up to my knee and nearly lost my balance. Victoria reached out and steadied me. I thought I would lose a boot in the sucking mud, but managed to pull free. I backtracked, and led us around the quagmire. "Remy," I finally answered, "Last Call is a day or two, at most."

"Black diamonds used to be mined in Last Call, right? Was that their source?" Remy asked.

"Yes. They may also come from the source of the Bimi," I replied, and I kept putting one foot in front of the other. Every step brought us closer to our ultimate destination.

"I don't care about diamonds or the sources of the Bimi," Koppes said. "We are walking through an amazing ecosystem. Take this cycad," she said, pointing at a nearby leafy purple fern. Stepping closer, she twisted a frond upside down, rubbed it, and took a deep breath.

I tried to preempt her. "Let me guess. It's a parasite."

"Correct." She broke a stem and squeezed a drop of pale lemon yellow sap from it. "This is amber in its liquid form. Every plant and animal has a version of this in their circulatory systems. It can be opaque or cloudy. It can be cherry red, gold, orange, or shades of purple. The color varies depending on the animal or plant, but they all have it. Amber is literally the lifeblood of the world."

"Maybe so," I said, "but black diamonds give rise to diamond root plants, and they are Nouveau Haitiah's flesh and bones." I grinned. My mentor, The Grand Maestro Alihak, would have been proud of me. Just then, a gust of wind brought the first heavy drops of rain. Large drops splattered the canopy and pelted my head. The noise made it difficult to follow the conversation. Victoria spoke, Remy said something, and Koppes answered.

"What?" I shouted, and stepped closer to Koppes.

324

"Parasites," she said loudly. "Micro-organisms."

Another thunderclap- I missed some of what she said-

"... In the lungs they complete their life cycle by releasing a hormone which drives the host to seek water."

Another peal of thunder- a natural symphony of dramatic sound-

"-filled with clear fluid which allows minimal oxygen/carbon dioxide exchange, sufficient to keep the host alive. The paralyzed host, nearly motionless and unable to speak, neither living nor dead-"

"Like a zombie?" Remy's eyes were wide with concern. The rain started coming down in sheets.

"Exactly," Koppes said.

Remy's mouth dropped open.

Koppes maintained a steady, thoughtful gaze. The soaked curls of her long red hair clunk to her cheeks and neck in matted tendrils. She could not keep it up and burst out laughing. "I'm kidding, Remy."

"Let's unpack the tarp and take shelter until this stops," I said.

It came down hard, and I watched a shallow circular puddle form next to the tarp. Raindrops splashed and made miniature fountains. They existed for a moment, too short-lived to be remembered, with each tiny fountain immediately replaced by another splashing drop. Soon, the rain abated, and only the occasional single drop fell into the puddle. The rippling concentric rings pleased me. The rainwater was so clear; I could make out each leaf and frond and twig on the bottom of the puddle. My mind attempted to impose order upon it, imagining letters and even words spelled in the forest floor detritus; but I could extract no meaning from nature, and so closed my eyes and rested.

Once the rain let up, we repacked the tarp and continued our march. The jungle felt like a sauna, and the footing was wet and treacherous. For mile after mile, my footsteps squelched through ocher mud. After a while, we came upon the low berm which formed the Bimi's bank, and the slightly higher ground made for easier walking, so we made good time. Last Call could not be much farther. I was tired. We were all tired. We grew careless. We spoke in loud voices, stepped on brittle sticks across the path, broke branches and pulled down vines, and generally proceeded without a second thought. Warned by the noise, unseen creatures slid through the purple and yellow reeds and splashed into the river, rippling mats of water canopia. Other creatures of unknown size floated in the shallows. Only their eyes were visible, tracking us with blank amphibian calculation.

We trekked into the hinterland of Nouveau Haitiah, paralleling the Bimi's course. Eventually, the low ridge flattened back into swamp. We crossed slow flowing tributaries using makeshift rafts constructed from bamboo analogs. Some of the stagnant backwaters were free of trees; instead, they were filled with turquoise steppingstone lilies, transforming waterways into living, floating meadows, and we crossed these ways by jumping from lily to lily.

The main channel eventually narrowed, and gradually changed from a flat, gunmetal gray to a clearer, flowing blue-green hue. That afternoon, I witnessed an astounding sight: a seething mass of white whips formed a living barrier stretching across the Bimi. I indulged in gloomy memories of Fernal and his untimely fate as well as my own encounter, but soon my thoughts returned to the goal of my quest.

Each evening we made camp and, conditions permitting, lit a fire. Dinners consisted of a monotonous diet of rice, red beans, and limes. At night, we slept on a tarp or improvised hammocks. Sleeping on the ground was not an option because of the annies.

Mile after mile, step after step, I led the way, chopping hose vines and brushing aside low purple fronds and sprawling thorn trees. Large-leafed dull violet shrubs exuded a pungent odor on contact. Koppes took pleasure in pointing out examples of various flora and fauna. Some creatures could be dangerous, such as the enormous pink and yellow arachnomoths which fluttered high in the canopy. They appeared benign, but the dust from their wings induced paralysis. Other creatures, such as skorpions, were as large as a loaf of bread and looked menacing, but were actually shy and harmless to humans. In any case, I made a point of keeping my machete and the ceramic grenades on my belt readily accessible.

We passed a children's fruit tree, and Koppes picked two heavy yellow fruits. She gave one to me, and took a bite from her own. "They are not actually fruits," she said. "They provide a good illustration of convergent evolution."

"What is that?" Remy asked.

"If you ask her questions," I said to Remy, "you will just encourage her to give you another lecture."

Koppes ignored me and explained convergent evolution to Remy; how similar environments created similar selective pressures, and therefore resulted in similar "morphologies."

Remy looked puzzled. "Morphologies?" I slapped my forehead with my palm. Remy gave me a dirty look. He really wanted to know.

I took a bite of my fruit. It tasted like vanilla, but it was too sweet. Although it contained microscopic parasites that took years to mature within a mock mynah, it was safe for humans to eat; however, children's fruit provided no nutrients my body could use. I coughed to clear my lungs, and took a deep breath to clear my head. I felt compelled to continue on my quest. I wanted to reach the source of the Bimi, and dwelling on the flora was a distraction from my goal.

The next day, Koppes led the march. We spent the better part of the morning slashing through a dank kane field. That afternoon consisted of another long slog through puddles, with mud occasionally up to my knees. Progress was both slow and exhausting. Heat, humidity, and arachnoflies continued to plague us, and brambles snagged our clothes. Several times we heard the low explosive chucks of a crapaud bouga in the distance.

The trail dried again, for which I was thankful. At one point, Koppes raised her hand for us to stop. "Octopede," she said, pointing to a pile of dead leaves on one side of the jungle floor. One of the leaves turned out to be a long, tubular, mottled brown creature the size of my foot. It emerged from the pile, scurried across our path, and disappeared into the brush. The lower portions of its body were rows of undulating legs. "It's harmless, but it can give a nasty bite," Koppes explained.

"All those legs give me the creeps," Remy said.

"It is a good example of the orientation of Nouveau Haitian life around the number eight. The octopede has eight bunches of eight legs each."

"That is a lot of legs," Remy said, nodding sagely. I am pretty sure he did not know any math.

"Two cubed times two cubed," Koppes explained. She thought she was being helpful.

A loud snap from nearby brush caught our attention. Koppes raised her hand in a warning gesture. Remy, Victoria, and I halted behind her. "I heard something," she said.

"There's a toad out there somewhere," Remy said, shifting from foot to foot and wringing his hands. We were all nervous. We continued with our machetes drawn.

Koppes was in front again. Her long red hair was a tangled mess, and her khaki long sleeve shirt and long pants were sopping wet. We penetrated a dark grove draped in long hanging curtains of ohm's moss. The moss created a tickling sensation whenever it came into contact with my skin. I did not mind because the moss kept away the arachnoflies.

As I slogged along the path, I thought about my goal. Korpusant once said "I dreamed about a Fountain of Youth." There had always been stories about the Fountain. Some suggested the childlike appearance of Odette and the lost people at Last Call meant the Fountain might be at the headwaters of the Bimi. Korpusant's dream about the Fountain back at Bois Caiman had been re-affirmed during my séance with Victoria. It had passed from the realm of dreams and stories to waking visions, from the realm of spoken lies to the realm of higher truth. I sought the Fountain of Youth!

I coughed again. It felt like I had fluid building up in my lungs.

What would happen if I found it? I was not sure.
Perhaps it would stop the ageing process and make
me immortal. Perhaps it would literally make me
young again. Naturally, I would share my discovery
with others. I entertained elaborate fantasies about
saving people, saving Victoria, followed by profuse
thanks and professions of love, and so on.

Lost in thought, I brushed aside a strand of ohm's
moss. The electrical tingle barely registered. I felt
compelled to push on, to reach my goal. The muggy
monotony of the hike through the sweltering jungle,
the oppressive, suffocating heat, the moist air, and the
repetitive hacking and slashing and trudging
continued.

We made our way through a long wet stretch where
the path was bracketed by black and yellow brambles,
with Koppes in the lead, followed by me, Victoria, and
Remy. Koppes chopped through a thick hose vine. A
stream of water from the cut gushed into her face,
temporarily blinding her and throwing her off balance.
Her knife fell into a shallow puddle as she flailed her
arms, staggering and splashing to one side. At that

moment, an enormous form crashed through the brambles. Taking advantage of the camouflage provided by its amber and black crosshatching, and using its native intelligence, the timing of the crapaud bouga's ambush proved devastatingly effective; in one hop, it was upon her.

Using its size and momentum, the eight-legged toad knocked her down and, before anyone could react, crushed her torso with it powerful plated jaws. She opened her mouth to scream, but instead of sound, a fountain of dark blood gushed forth.

I rushed to aid the scientist. Unhooking a ceramic grenade from my belt and pulling the pin, I shoved it under the toad's huge belly, and jumped back. The explosion showered me with pink jellied gobs.

Ears ringing, I returned to stand over the body of Koppes, joined by Remy and Victoria. The scientist lay motionless in the mud, her eyes unseeing. The crapaud bouga's body, essentially several hundred pounds of watery flesh, had been shredded by the grenade. Its huge head was still intact, and its jaws remained clamped upon her crushed torso.

Incredibly, its black unblinking eyes tracked my every movement. Reaching down, I attempted to pry apart the plated jaws, but without success. They were locked in a death grip. The predator was inseparable from the prey.

Remy opened and closed his mouth, but no words came out. Tears ran down Victoria's face. "What are we going to do?" she asked in a choked voice.

I focused on the enormous, warty head of the crapaud bouga, and stared into its intelligent black eyes. The toad stared back. Its jaws worked slightly back and forth, readjusting its grip upon its prey. I buried my face in my hands. What were we to make of the way an intelligent creature behaved in its dying moment?

LAST CALL

The left fork of the once powerful river now amounted to little more than a sluggish creek. The further we progressed, the more sinister the landscape appeared. Milky water seeped past weedy banks, where dry purple and yellow reeds struggled to survive on random patches of black sand. Portions of the banks were covered with slippery, liver hued splotches of slime, and in other places, a dull blue mold clung to the clay. Fumaroles spewed foul smelling clouds.

My urge to find the source became more and more urgent, but the forbidding landscape seemed to embody disappointment; it was an almost physical betrayal of my instinctive desire.

"We should have taken the other fork," I said to Victoria, and coughed to clear my lungs. The need to clear them was becoming more frequent. I thought it was a respiratory infection. In addition, my pack chafed my shoulders. I adjusted the straps without even thinking about it.

"We've come this far. Maybe we should go a little farther," Victoria said. "We know something bad happened at Last Call. This," she said, indicating the water, "might be part of it." She knelt by the stream and dipped in a finger, and touched it to her lips. "I don't like the taste of this."

It was good to hear Victoria speak. Since the death of Koppes, she had been uncharacteristically subdued and prone to bursting into tears. I am sure she cared about Koppes, but other than their both being intelligent women, they shared little in common. I think Victoria shed tears because she was shocked by how quickly it happened, by the overwhelming violence and the quantity of blood, and by the sheer randomness of the attack. Of course, part of it was also due to exhaustion and another part to uncertainty over the outcome of this journey. At least she had the decency not to blame me for the grenade, which might have killed the scientist if she had not already been mortally injured.

I tried the water too. It tasted wrong. "Don't drink from the stream, Remy. Only drink from your canteen."

"I didn't drink any," Remy said. That was not true. I saw him drink from the polluted stream several times. "Let's keep going," he said. "The diamonds are close now." He showed traces of his old enthusiasm when he thought about the black diamonds, but most of the time he remained silent, and fingered his amber dice.

At this point, Victoria seemed to be in better physical shape than me or Remy, so she led for the next two days. She cleared brittle kanes using loose swings of her black diamond machete. Remy and I followed. We trudged along a path of packed dirt which skirted fields of grey bubbling mud pots. Fumaroles occurred more often, and the smell of rotten eggs became pervasive. We passed magnificent rainbow colored pools of superheated hot springs, deep blue in their centers with edges rimmed in rings of amber and apricot.

At times we picked up the original road to Last Call. Its shoulders were occasionally bordered by small piles of rubble; they were all that remained of the memento mori erected by the townspeople a long time ago. Faded bits of once-colorful ribbon were scattered amid the stones. Nothing whatsoever could be deduced from the piles of rocks about the subjects of the memorials.

After more hiking, the reeds and weeds beneath our feet gave way to low patches of sparkling purple leaves- diamond root. The Bimi now flowed to my left, little more than a creek. We entered a large clearing, and once again the sulfurous reek of rotten eggs filled the air.

"Last Call," Victoria said.

Before us stood a rickety gate set in a low palisade of bone white wood. It was unlatched, so I pushed it open; when I pushed, it fell off its wooden hinges. I stepped into the compound, followed by Remy and Victoria. The wooden wall encircled a flat open area, and a few tilting structures still stood around the perimeter. Within the abandoned confines, no plant graced the area. It was completely barren. The ground and all of the roofs of the dilapidated buildings

were covered by a thin, off-white mineral crust. I
called several times. No one answered.

As I walked towards the center of the compound, each
footstep broke through the thin mineral rime with a
crunch. On the opposite side, a series of mineral
terraces formed irregularly layered steps in concentric
rings, leading to a small gray cone in the center.
Steam rose from it and from several nearby vents.
The sulfurous odor permeated the entire compound.
From underground came a low, almost imperceptible
rumble.

Remy took a step towards the mound. Victoria
grabbed him by an arm and pulled him back. The
gesture reminded me of the time on the Santeria
when Koppes pulled me back to keep me from
jumping after Fernal.

"Hey!" Remy yelled. "What are you doing?"

"Don't go any closer," she replied.

"Why not?"

"You might break through the crust and get scalded."

The subsurface churning and rumbling grew louder. Steam poured from vents surrounding the cone, and boiling water surged from its apex, to cascade down the terraces in flat, torrential liquid sheets. A fountain of water and steam shot high in the air, its hot mist enveloping us.

I pumped my fist in the air. "I did it! I have found it!" Remy reached for me, but I eluded his grasp and rushed towards the geyser, heedless of danger, shouting for joy. Victoria made no attempt to stop me.

I focused upon the fountain of steam and water to the exclusion of all else. My feet cracked the brittle surface, and I paused, exulting in the ecstasy of the moment. Laughing, I tore off my ragged shirt, and let the hot fine mist shower down upon me.

"Remy! Victoria! This is wonderful! Come here!"

Remy stood stock still, gaping in astonishment. "Are you out of your mind?"

Roaring with triumphant laughter, I bathed in the geyser mists, rubbing myself vigorously. I held my arms perpendicular to the ground and spun in a circle with my head tilted back, and let the fine droplets fall into my open mouth.

The smell and taste of sulfur brought me back to my senses. On one hand, the water felt good, like a refreshing warm bath; on the other hand, I did not feel youthful or rejuvenated. I just felt... wet.

Pulse by pulse, the geyser plume lessened, until the eruption ceased. Hot water continued pouring down the natural steps, ferrying tiny stones down the terraces. A jet black object the size of an egg tumbled along with the flow, and bumped my foot. I picked it up. The object was a black diamond. I closed my fist around it, and carried it back to Remy and Victoria.

"What's wrong with you?" Remy asked. "Are you crazy?"

Without a word, I extended my hand to Remy and opened my fist. The black diamond seemed to absorb the sunlight into itself. I gave it to him.

Remy's eyes widened. He whooped and crushed me in an embrace. When I did not respond, he pulled back, puzzled by my lack of excitement. "Come on! We've done it! We found the black diamonds!"

I closed my eyes and hung my head, slowly shaking it from side to side. My disappointment was devastating.

Victoria knew. She put her hands on her hips and faced me. "You were always after more than black diamonds, weren't you? Tell Remy why you dragged him all the way here."

"What could be more important than black diamonds?" Remy asked.

Victoria answered for me: "The Fountain of Youth."

I looked Remy in the eye and nodded. "It is true."

"What!" Remy clenched his hands into fists. Breathing even harder than usual, he stood right in front of me. "I came all this way for that? I risked my life!"

My emotions overwhelmed me and I could not speak. What could I possibly say? I looked away.

"I trusted you. You lied."

"That is not entirely true, Remy," Victoria said. "We also came to find out if the black diamond trade could be re-opened. We succeeded. The diamonds are still here." I was surprised she came to my defense. "We also know," Victoria continued, "this geyser erupted within the perimeter of Last Call. This might be why they stopped mining. Maybe the mines flooded, or maybe the geyser water poisoned the crops and forced everyone out."

We all pondered this in silence. Victoria was right, of course. She surveyed the compound and made a sweeping gesture of her arm. "The geyser is flushing the diamonds onto the open ground. There may be a whole layer of them beneath this mineral crust."

Remy rubbed his chin. Victoria knew how to capture his interest.

"There is something else to consider," I said. "All of the stories point to the possibility that The Fountain of Youth, or at any rate, something extraordinary, may exist at the head of the Bimi. That might be worth more than all the black diamonds in Last Call."

"Maybe," Remy said reluctantly.

Victoria narrowed her eyes and puckered her lips as she considered this.

"We should keep going," I said. "Look at how small the Bimi has become. The source must be close. We have enough supplies. Let's go." I did not think it would help my case to mention the only reason we had enough supplies was because Koppes had died, and we had added hers to our own; instead, I decided to force the issue. I felt bad about lying to Remy. Lying was a form of betrayal. But I *wanted* to go, and no degree of disappointment would make me quit, and nothing they could say would dissuade me. I coughed to clear my lungs, and then turned and walked towards the gate with purposeful strides.

"It's too dangerous," Remy said behind me. "I don't see the point." He rubbed his hands across his face. "I don't feel good."

Victoria sighed. She was frustrated with both of us. Still, she managed to address him with kindness. "Come on, Remy. We should stick together. Besides, he is right; the source of this branch of the Bimi must be close." She took his hand, and they followed me

out the gate of Last Call, and back into a desolate
landscape.

THE YEW

We followed the left fork of the Bimi along its weedy banks through sickly savannahs of wilted yellow xanthia grass. Normally the grass grew to eye level, but here it only grew knee-high and stretched listlessly across a sere, rolling country. The dry grass swayed with the occasional puff of wind, which spread a rancid redolence. After a day's walk along the gray clay bank even the xanthia grass disappeared, though its smell still permeated my clothing. The forlorn creek became a trickle, and at last, we came to a vast, desolate field. Nothing grew. No living creature inhabited the wide and empty space. The milky trickle terminated at the base of an enormous leafless tree, which occupied the center of the blasted field. Twisted roots spread from the trunk and then dove into the ground, as if seeking to strangle the world's center. High, bare branches seemed to weave themselves into the pale violet overcast, while a thick and putrid liquid emanated from its bole. Even from a distance, I could see the milky sap emerging from ancient wounds in the gnarled trunk, like a fountain flowing in slow motion. This flow gathered on the ground in a small, egg-shaped pool, to form a beginning- a source- of the Bimi.

I sighed, which brought on another coughing fit. After all the risks, after the peril of the river and the jungle, after the brutal deaths of Fernal, Franklin, Galvani, and Koppes, after all that, I now came to stand here in the midst of a poisonous wasteland, and I stated the obvious: "This is not the Fountain of Youth." My shoulders slumped, and I shook my head in wonder. "This is the origin? This is the source of the Bimi?"

"There is no Fountain," Remy said, making no effort to hide his bitterness. "There never was. The black diamonds were real, but here we are, and they are back at Last Call."

"I refuse to accept this." I turned to Victoria. "What is this?"

She waved her hand at the tree. "It's a Nouveau Haitian yew."

"I don't believe it. That is something from folklore."

Victoria raised her eyebrows. "Folklore? Really?" She pointed at the tree. "Then what do you call that?"

"It is not a yew tree. There is no such thing."

"It makes perfect sense," she insisted. "This explains what happened to the people of Last Call. This also explains Odette's poisons."

"What happened in Last Call?" Remy asked. He was still worrying about the diamonds.

"This tree must have taken root at the head of the Bimi and contaminated the water supply. The water would have grown more and more toxic."

"Maybe it killed the adults first," I guessed. "Children might have been less susceptible. They formed The Children's Fund."

"At some point that geyser in Last Call might have flooded the mines," Victoria said. "Maybe that was the last blow."

"It could have happened after the water was poisoned." I coughed and spat clear fluid.

"That is why you are coughing," Remy said. "I don't feel good either."

I had been coughing before we encountered the poisoned water, but I had a more immediate concern. "We can do something about this," I said, unsheathing my machete. "Remy, help me." Brandishing my knife, I strode towards the trunk of the tree. Remy immediately understood my intent, and followed.

We hacked at the bark with our razor sharp machetes for a long time and worked off our frustration. The edges of the knives cut into the bark, but the trunk was so big around, it looked like we had made almost no progress. In addition, we had to be extremely careful not to come into contact with the poisonous sap that oozed from the bark, the water that formed a small stream at its base, and the dangerous droplets that flew from the cut as we chopped.

Remy and I stood back and assessed our effort. The tree still stood. Perhaps our assault had dealt the giant yew a fatal blow, but I doubted it. We were exhausted and drenched with sweat. "Never mind that," I said to Remy. I led him a safe distance away from the trunk. "Here, help me." I unhooked a ceramic grenade from my belt, and handed him one as well. I lobbed it at the base of the blighted tree. Remy tossed another. Each grenade detonated with a blast, peppering the gray bark with ceramic shrapnel. The grenades were not nearly powerful enough to knock down the tree, but they might harm it, and if nothing else, I thought a few explosions might cheer us up.

Victoria stood a short distance away with her arms crossed. "Had enough?" Remy and I grinned by way of reply. "Then we have to leave," she continued. "This is a poisonous place."

We turned and walked away from the yew in sober silence. After a while, Victoria spoke. "The yew is the source of the Bimi. Poison is the lifeblood of the world."

"Odette was right all along," Remy added.

"No," I said. "I don't believe it. I don't believe this is the true source of the Bimi."

"What do you mean?" Victoria asked. "We were all there. You saw it."

"I know," I said slowly, "but it does not feel right. This is only one source. There is another fork. There must be more than this. We will go back and trace the river's other fork, the right fork. We will find the true source."

THE FOUNTAIN

Victoria stopped and raised her hand in the air. "Wait. I need to catch my breath." She halted halfway up the grassy slope and put her hands on her knees, gasping.

"I must find the Fountain," I said. My instinctual urge drove me on. Nothing would stop me from answering the call of the Bimi's truer source- not Victoria, not Remy, not even the fluid in my lungs. We seemed to be on the right track. This fork flowed clear and cold and the foliage flourished along the banks in a profusion of purples, lilacs, lavenders, and violets. Diamond root hugged the ground, covering the floor beneath the bushes, ferns, and occasional cycads, and its anise and old campfire odor filled the air.

"Let's go," I said. Victoria ignored me. She spread out the tarp, and she sat upon it. Remy lay upon it and curled into a fetal position.

"Remy cannot go any further," Victoria said. She was right. Remy was extremely ill. He was tired, increasingly withdrawn, and uncharacteristically introspective. He was sick to his stomach with

increasing frequency and his strength had given out. I
feared he would not leave this place, but I tried to
sound upbeat when I asked him the question anyway.
"How are you feeling?"

"Bad. I feel so tired. You're a doctor. Can you save
me?"

I pointed to the higher ground ahead of us. "The
Fountain is somewhere up there. Maybe it will cure
you. Don't you want to try?"

"Yes, if it is there." He moaned. "I can't go any
farther."

"Maybe Victoria and I can bring the water back to
you."

"I will stay with Remy," Victoria said. "I cannot
abandon him." Her eyes were wide and teary, but she
did not cry. She took a deep breath. "I will not leave
his side; not even for The Fountain of Youth, if it is up
there. We will wait for you here." I was taken aback
by this amazing demonstration of loyalty and
compassion and sacrifice on the part of Victoria. I
recalled a vision in a crystal ball of Victoria in old age,

combing her hair before a mirror. I am sure she remembered, too; she knew- *she knew*- she was giving away her chance to bathe in the Fountain of Youth; she was one of the vainest people I had ever met, yet she would give up the prospect of eternal youth in order to stay by Remy's side.

I should have stayed with them, but I could not. I was drawn. I was driven.

"Let me stay here on the tarp," Remy blurted. "Don't let the annies get me."

"He's right," Victoria said. "Let us keep the tarp. Remy can rest on it. How long should we wait for you?"

I shrugged. "A day or two, I suppose. If you are not here when I return, I will catch up with you."

Remy extended his hand towards me. He held something in it. "Take this with you."

"*Merci.*" He dropped the object into my open palm. I was sure it would be the large black diamond we found at Last Call. I thought the diamond would be the thing he valued the most, and he would give it to me. I am ashamed to say this- I underestimated Remy- because he did not give me the diamond. He gave me his favorite pair of amber dice. We all knew we might not see each other again. I left my backpack and everything except my canteen with them. I hugged Victoria and shook Remy's hand. We said our good-byes.

I trotted up the gentle slope, alone, upbeat, and focused, and conducting myself in a manner worthy of a Valedictorian or The Grand Maestro. Once I paused and pulled out Remy's gift. I rubbed the octagonal dice with my thumb and felt the amber's electrical current. It was time to roll. I continued upslope, and my determined stride soon turned into a headlong rush. I no longer bothered to follow the river bank, instead crashing in a straight line through the luxuriant foliage. I could not stop. I could not help myself. Coughing to clear my lungs again, I plunged through a thick stand of tall fern analogs without slowing. I crossed the Bimi again, and walked up the clear stream, splashing with each step, no longer caring where my feet fell. I passed a grove of thin yellow trees, and then strode across solid ground again and up a hill.

The landscape blurred with my memories. Thunderheads piled up on the horizon, their color so intense, they bordered on the ultraviolet. That distant line of towering cumulonimbus looked like the clouds above the Phosphor Plain, so long ago. I remembered a field of yellow spear grass at twilight, and watching eight-legged lightning bugs, tiny blue flashing points of luminescence, hovering over the meadow like miniature blue stars, darting about and dancing to a natural music of the spheres. I remembered blue beetles, metallic red arachnoflies, and a mollymander spouting in the middle of the Bimi.

I scrambled up the slope of the brown hill; I scrambled up the slope of my memories. My last ecstatic memories after being shocked by a white whip and nearly drowning came back in full force. The white whip parasites and the water of the Bimi became a part of me that day, and they now drove me to this final and ultimate affirmation, this personal migration to the source. Ahead, a small musical waterfall tumbled from the hill's brow, and reeds grew around its brim. I ran for the top, gasping for breath, lungs filling with liquid. The melodic falling sound of the waterfall made me frantic with desire- more than anything, I wanted to forge ahead, go over the brim, and once and for all, find the source of my salvation and redemption.

I climbed the slick gray rocks to the edge of waterfall, and at last, achieved the summit. I felt drawn to the circular, dust covered pool on the other side, and said aloud in a bemused voice: "It seems the soul really does migrate to water." And I dove in.

Dedicated to my mother

Fran McEwing

Special thanks to my Editor, Sarah McEwing; Illustrator
and creator of the cover, Julia Thummel; and
Webmaster Jennifer Howells. Also to my wife and first
reader, Virginia. I would also like to thank my high
school English teachers- Helen Warren, Bill Menza,
and Marjorie Hicks- and friend Paul Guay for being
supportive all these years. And finally, a big thank you
to the members of the AOL Mindflight critique group
from the late 90's and early 00's, including Amy
Sterling Casil.

See www.nouveauhaitiah.com for cool illustrations,
more about *Nouveau Haitiah*, news on upcoming

books and stories including *Ghosts from the Mountains of Madness* (2016), critical essays, and biographical information. Topics include speculative fiction, science fiction, Proust, Haiti, modernism, and anthropology.

Proof